Khantara

Volume One

Also by Michelle Franklin

Tales from Frewyn: The Opera & The Reporter from Marridon

Khantara

Volume One

KHANTARA

A Haanta Series Novel
By Michelle Franklin
Art by Twisk

Khantara

Volume One

A Haanta Series Novel
By Michelle Franklin
Art by Twisk

For Sheenah:

The subdued warrior who trundles through the sludge of literary woes to discover all its lost endearing joys.

Table of Contents

This novel comes with a free ebook copy!

To receive, go to http://bit.ly/13qqJpd
And use the code FREEBIE
The ebook will be emailed to you within 24 hours.

He Who Moves Like Shadow

new leader had come to power in Thellis, the largest nation on the northern mainland of the Two Continents, and in a fit of imprudence and brash resolve, the first declaration he made to mark out his rule was to launch an attack upon their longstanding rivals. Many thought this an ill-advised action, but the magisters' pleas in the Thellisian Parliament went unheeded and Thellis would war with the Haanta. Their first aim was the island of Sanhedhran, the Haanta main island, one of trade and commerce, and though this island held the chief of their people and their armed forces, Thellis' target this time would be Mhavhaledhran, the Haanta judiciary island where its leaders and military heads were said to reside. Although the Haanta and Thellis had been warring for the better part of the last few hundred years, making the Haanta ever on the watch for a fresh assault, they had not expected such an unprecedented assailment after the last retaliation they had accorded. It resulted in the death of Thellis' previous leader, not from any attack the Haanta could make, but one from the strain and stress of a heart worn by ceaseless conflict.

Though the war between the rivaling nations had been long, the recent series of battles had been short; the conflict had begun just as it always had done: Thellis began it with their massive fleets and magic weaponry, and the Haanta had ended it with their superior might, immense size, and insurmountable designs. Thellis, however, could not be satisfied with defeat after having spent so much time and effort toward breaking the Haanta's impenetrable defenses; they must find means of reprisal with the few resources they had remaining to salvage their pride and boast of at least a partial victory.

And so, the newly elected Emperor of Thellis, a small man of obdurate character and blinding resolve, sent his men to Mhavhaledhran with the object of destroying the Haanta temple, hoping that such a desecration of their home would yield their surrender. This plan might have been enough to bend the Haanta conviction, but Thellis' advance, though slender, had been calculated and had been partially subdued. The soldiers were simple enough for the Haanta to dispatch, but the numerous magi were another matter. Although the Haanta had their own magi capable of boundless destruction, their abilities were unstable and the use of their talents was therefore ill-advised. The Haanta would have to check the assault without the use of magic, and though lives would be lost, they would die gloriously in the throes of battle with honour and with purpose.

Once the Thellisian magi came to the shores of Mhavhaledhran, the Hakriyaa, the Haanta military leader, ordered the initiation of their vicious retribution. Hundreds of the giant warriors poured forth from the shore and hundreds more surrounded them, striking at the magi from behind. It was an unfortunate loss for Thellis, for all of their men had died and were sent back in their ships to be buried in their homeland. The Haanta temple on Mhavhaledhran had been spared, but the affront of being invaded was too great. Something must be done to convey the Haanta's insulted sentiments, and the Hakriyaa would make them understand that should Thellis choose to stand on their shores uninvited once again, the race of giants would not restrain themselves when forced to revisit the mainland. To quell Thellis' penchant for war, the Hakriyaa deployed a battalion of one-thousand Haanta Amghari, the collected warriors from across the northern archipelago, to venture to the mainland and overpower the easternmost settlements of Thellis. Thellis would be expecting an assault upon their capital in the west, but here their ambitions would be unfulfilled and they forced to traverse the far reaches of their nation to defend against such an incursion, a retaliation that would take time to plan, and it was here that the Haanta would establish themselves on the mainland for the first time since their arrival to the islands.

The regiment of one-thousand mountainous men was led by the supreme commander of Mhavhaledhran, the Den Amhadhri Khantara, the largest of the western Haanta ever recorded. At nine feet, the giant of giants soared over his men, governing them with firm but quiet words, gathering them into their formations and commanding them onto their ships across the slender reaches of the Northern Sea. Khantara had lived to lead many wars against their one adversary and could boast of much success as a commander, but he chose reservation and quietude though his people remarked him as a transcendent and reverential figure. Many gifts were accorded the quiet and peaceable giant, and though handsomeness was not one of them, where he failed in prepossessing appearances he succeeded in ability. He was an Amghari of the highest decoration. His large two-handed axe boasted the extent of all his ambition, and though he had talent for tactics and battle, he relished being unspoken and reserved. He favoured observation and his powers of attending over speaking, and though not the most ardent of orators, when the mammoth did venture to speak, everyone around him listened. He preferred his communications of the Sotaa, or the Hunter's

Gift: the talent for conversing with animals without the hindrance of words. Delighting in his inbred ability, especially when crossing the Northern Sea, his mind was a constant commotion of messages passing to and from the nature around him, from the birds chirping about seeds they just found to fish beckoning one another to form schools. Attending to every one of the voices kept him tranquil and quiet throughout the short journey, for listening and learning from their wordless communication was all his perfect serenity.

It could not be denied that war was something Khantara did rather well, though he had little taste for battle. Overshadowing and overpowering others was an easy office for him to fulfill, and he often preferred allowing his opponents to escape rather than using the extent of his immense strength to subdue them. Even a challenger in a friendly match of Hophsaas would submit to his enormous size and unrelenting might. All of the Amghari and Amhadhri, warriors and commanders beneath his station, bowed to him and obeyed him with honour, calling him Odaibha, a master in all things, and many flocked to him in hopes of gleaning a few morsels of his wisdom and catching the few tender words he cared to utter. They watched his every action with great interest, marked his every move on the field, and due to the attention and adulation Khantara incurred, he often sought the comforts of solitude and silence whenever it was permitted him.

While Khantara may have been foreboding in stature, he was kindly in countenance. His long grey and molded locks acquitted him of tidiness, his yellow irises and black sclera gave him an air of uncommon penetration, his dark grey and stone-like skin boasted of a life spent in training, but his cloak, long and black, sleek and draping, made him seem a walking shadow. His shadowcloak, or Dhanna, was comprised of a heavy, form-fitting silk called Bhastaatsa, a fabric fashioned on the islands and never traded away to the neighboring nations. Meant for the islands' informants, the garment was useful for guarding against the heavy rains that plagued the islands for months together and aided Khantara in hiding his mountainous form when light was scarce. His adoration for his cloak granted him name of Vhessehl Dhoss-hi, He who Moves like Shadow, a title much preferred by Khantara and much more agreeable than He who Conquers, as his Amghari designation had suggested.

He had been named as Den Amhadhri when he was only nine and had been taken to be trained in seclusion with an Odaibha of his own for many years. His dark grey skin had been abraded every season to ensure its durability, his hair had been bound to maintain its vast length, when the Hakriyaa honoured him with his axe upon his instatement, the name of Khantara was given him with the hopes that he would be their glorious conqueror, despite his desire for peacefulness and isolation. Enjoying his new name had little to do with satisfying expectations; where Khantara was bid to lead, there he did go, dutifully following the order of his superior, but always acting with prudence and respect with regard to his command. Khantara was soon a name of legend across the northern archipelago, a name of a learned and sagacious creature who sought more to teach than he did to make war. All his happiness was in instructing the young Mivaari of the islands; the Haanta children enjoyed his quiet manner and reticent company, and the summoning of animals for their edification only expiated their interest and delight. He was attentive to their skills and watched them closely as they developed, doing much through action and less through word, as he understood that children must be shown and not told if they are to retain what they have learned. He adored his students and harboured a secretive wish to one day nurture his own Mivaari without the Themari's interference. Such a desire, however, must be unfounded; one-hundred years he had defended and edified his people, and the continued attacks from Thellis would keep him from realizing his one humble aspiration. He did, however, have those in his command whom he regarded as his own: three Amhadhri whom he had nurtured and trained since their childhood followed everywhere since the day he was named as their teacher. They were forever in his shadow, awaiting their Odaibha's command, and all Khantara's affection and pride was for how well they had grown and how skilled in their arts they had become. They were given their own ships and regiments of Amghari to command, and once the Haanta fleet neared the northern shores of Thellis, they were given the order not to strike the mainland's inhabitants no matter how poorly their arrival and occupation of their land should be received.

When their ships docked and Khantara disembarked, he walked with a slow and shuffling gait and garnered much attention, gaining bows and words of praise and supplication from every one of his blessed people and from those he was about to peaceably conquer. His stride was small for a man of his height, giving him time to judge the confounded Thellisians with civility. He could not but observe their wide eyes and their trembling forms as he approached to address them. He bowed to them, assured them that they were not here to harm them, but they would not attend; they were too fixed on the giant's gargantuan form and immense army to hear his explanation. He noted a few Thellisians leave the congregation, possibly to warn others of their coming, but he knew that this must follow and hoped that in time their two nations could find means of living in tolerable peace.

He gave orders to begin creating an outpost, a place where the Haanta would reside and watch over the activities of their enemy. There was no blood to be shed, as those in the Thellisian settlement had surrendered without opposition, and the Amghari were commanded to guard the vanquished while ships bearing more of the Haanta people were sent for. Masons and carpenters were brought to begin work on their temple and homes, tradesmen and merchants were conveyed to erect stalls in the marketplace, clothiers and provisioners were employed to bring their wares, and within a few days of their arrival, the Haanta had created a supportable home.

The three Amhadhri, however, soon grew concerned for Khantara's wellbeing: he oversaw the erection of the Haanta homes and the temple, assisted those who came to settle in the new outpost to give it life and culture, and helped the carpenters build the training grounds and barracks for his men. They asked if the giant was well, if he should like to rest and take refreshment, if he would not take a room in the temple for a few hours, but Khantara declined all such solicitude. He would take nothing and have no rest while the outpost was being built. Suggestions were made for him to honour their women with Khopra and help populate their new settlement with their young, but as Khantara had never honoured anyone with the Haanta's most sacred ritual, all offers were politely denied. He feared his size, weight and strength might be too much for one of their women to endure, and he decided that his exemption at Khopra was well deserved when his duties of Den Amhadhri and Odaibha were ever so much more consequential to perform at such a time. The three Amhadhri must be satisfied with their Odaibha's answer and only hoped that the settlement would be soon finished so that their teacher might find enjoyment in training the Amghari, instructing the Mivaari, and taking his long nightly walks once everything was arranged.

Only once during the erection of the Haanta settlement had the Thellisian forces come to expel them. It was natural that Thellis should wish to remove them; they were settling on their lands, occupying their people, and something must be done to destroy them. Thellis, however, was in no position to spare anymore of their forces from their capital; too many had died in the battle on Mhavhaledhran, their leader had been too precipitant to retaliate in the wake of the late emperor's death, the nation was ill-prepared for an invasion, but it was too late to reclaim their forces and only a few hundred had come to face one thousand giants. The Thellisian soldiers came to the front line of the Haanta settlement and laid down their spears; they did not wish to lose their lives and begged for kindness toward their people. Kindness was given and their lives were spared. They were sent back to the Thellisian capital to give a message to the new emperor: the Haanta intended to stay, and if Thellis would seek to remove them, they would retaliate without mercy. Thellis' numbers were too few to combat this point. They must allow the Haanta to have their way for the present while they fuss and officiate from the seat in Parliament, keeping an ever watchful eye on their close enemy and contriving manners in which to destroy them from within.

The Thellisian inhabitants of the settlement were left alone and were permitted to continue their lives as they would. Conversion to the Haanta faith and way of life was offered to all who wished it, but few came forward. Some of those who accepted the offer did so out of fear, but those who led a more deprived existence took the conversion as charity. This gave rise to claims that the Haanta had come to impose their culture upon them, and though this was hardly true in any respect, a few Thellisians rose against the Haanta and attacked their carpenters and masons to keep them from building their temple and homes. The rebellion was quickly dissolved: those who had harmed or even killed members of the Haanta collective were sent to a camp on Mhavhaledhran to serve small sentences of labour and solitude. It was a gentle punishment for so horrid an offense, but as the Thellisians saw the rebels being carted away with no notion of where they were going, rumours began to spread of enforced servitude. What was meant as an offer of continual peace had become a dreadful evil: where Khantara was once perceived as a peaceful conqueror, the mountainous leader was now seen as a warlord, offering peace as an excuse to send more Thellisians back to the islands as slaves; those who had joined the Haanta collective were seen as mere automatons living the falseness of a happy life under a cruel conviction; and those who refused to abide the Haanta presence banned the giants from their buildings, believing the Haanta tranquility to be a façade for a later assault, creating fences and partitions demarcating every area where Thellisian was allowed and Haanta was not. A needless divide was now between them, and all hopes of peace in the settlement were lost. Khantara was sorry that it had come to this; he had hoped for more than a few days of harmony between their two peoples, but he resigned himself to the consolation that things might be mended in time and his reputation amongst the Thellisians might yet be salvaged.

The outpost was now equally divided: temple, barracks and Haanta settlement on one side and Church and Thellisian dwellings on the other, but their common ground lay in the marketplace. There every Haanta was welcome to buy, sell, and trade wares. Many at first thought this acceptance untoward, but once they learned that the Haanta paid in bars of gold and silver, every merchant was eager to trade with them. The Haanta, however, were an affluent and self-sufficient race and were seldom seen near the Thellisian stalls, except when walking from their portion of the settlement to the docks to help those who came from the archipelago to further populate their new home. They claimed their own small section of the marketplace to welcome Thellisian and even Lucentian traders, to share in their well-made and valuable natural resources and commodities.

When the temple was nearly finished, a celebration was called in honour of Khantara and his tremendous efforts toward creating a home for his people on the mainland. The commemoration was to be held in the newly built celebration grounds beside the temple and everyone Thellisian and Haanta alike were invited. The Church of Thellis, however, believed the gracious invitation to be a trick of some kind and advised its parishioners not to attend, and those who were caught entering the celebration or even speaking to one of the giants were to be seen as one of them and asked to leave the Thellisian portion of the settlement. Some would disobey if only to quell their curiosities, most would remain at home and ignore the mellifluous music and lively dances, but all would agree not to grow too enamored with any of the rituals they might or might not observe.

At the beginning of the celebration, it was declared that the outpost was to be called Khantara Ghaasta, so named for its securer. Praise would be given him for his immense achievement, songs would be sung telling of his glory, and meals must be had with Khantara himself as the invited guest of honour. The colossus, however, had small heart for celebration: he felt as though he had achieved nothing by situating his people here. He had exposed them to greed, to fear, to cruelty, ideals which they had never hitherto known, and had subjected them to the caprice of their enemies when they would have otherwise been left alone on the safety of the islands. He went to the celebration only long enough for his people to feel honoured and short enough that he might slip away within the folds of his Dhanna before the dancing should begin to spend the rest of the evening ruminating over the consequence of what he had done.

His three Amhadhri, however, could not be pleased with his early departure. They noted his going and gave one another half glances of disconsolation. The smallest of the three, the

Amhadhri Jhiaanta, forever worried for his master's comfort, leapt after him as he walked down one of the proprietary lanes leading toward the Thellisian part of the settlement and entreated Khantara's consideration with a bow and a look of vexation.

"Odaibha," Jhiaanta pleaded. "Will you not join us for the remainder of the commemoration? It was made to honour you."

Khantara hummed in deliberation. He placed his massive hand on the commander's shoulder to convey his sentiments of appreciation but would not turn back toward the festivities.

Jhiaanta, so used to his master's blithesome disposition, became even more worried when Khantara did not treat his needless agitation with his usual assuring smile. "Are you not pleased, Odaibha?"

"I am," Khantara said in a low hum, making little effort to show his pleasance. "Let our people rejoice. I must walk."

Jhiaanta was desirous of knowing why his master was so troubled, and though he had many questions to ask on the subject, he checked himself and would obey his master's wish for solitude. He bowed, stepped back from the path and watched his master's shadow shuffle away.

Khantara was sensible of Jhiaanta's silent entreaties and resolved to answer him once time should furnish him with the tranquilization he sought. He considered why the Haanta were here in the outpost, he considered their future on the mainland and the allies they were perhaps to find here. Only once along his path did he stop to converse with birds of their newly made nests, and when he gained a few of the delicate and pleasant creatures for his shoulders, he continued along the lane, wrapped his shadowcloak about him, and vanished from view.

Unwilling to concede and unresolved in his suppositions, Jhiaanta moved to follow his master but was stopped by one of his brother Amhadhri.

"Leave our Odaibha, Jhiaanta," said the largest of the three commanders. "He has done his duty to us and more than deserves his isolation."

Jhiaanta looked back along the path where Khantara had been moments before. "I worry for him, Bhaaldhena," he sighed.

Bhaaldhena placed his hands on his hips and simpered, "You always do. It is your nature to worry. You would worry about the sky if you could."

"He will not be able to instruct the Mivaari until the temple is fully erected," Jhiaanta added, ignoring Bhaaldhena's mocking assertion. "He finds much comfort in teaching them and in training us." He looked toward the lights outlining the windows of Thellisian residences in the distance. "The continual rebellion of these Dhargovhari will upset him."

"Our master is hardly disturbed by anything, Jhiaanta. His size and composure affords him that." Bhaaldhena gestured toward the celebration grounds. "Come. Watch our women dance, enjoy the Abharaas, and leave our Odaibha to himself."

Jhiaanta made one more backward glance down the darkened lane, regarded the silent one of the three Amhadhri with a chary glance, and followed Bhaaldhena into the commemoration while the quiet third remained outside the celebration grounds, remarking his master's wake with austere concern.

THE WALK

lthough the sun was beginning to set over the outpost, and the chief of the prevailing light would soon be the fires of the celebration behind him and the dim hint of the luminaries above, Khantara's walk was well supplied with the echoing calls of nighthawks and the coos of owls to support his journey. This lane had become a favourite for his nightly walks: it was wide enough to house his immense form and slender enough that the gales from the nearby Eastern Sea could be caught between the copses of trees lining the path. Here was all his tranquility: in the sounds of rustling leaves and shivering boughs; in the cries of chicks calling out for their mother and in the swoop of the mother attending them; in the subdued scents of the unfamiliar flora around him, in their brilliant alloys and in the velvet texture of their petals. All his equanimity swiftly returned, and he blessed his surroundings for renewing his peace of mind and securing his solitude. He had only to walk, to remark, and to listen.

The nighthawks adorning his shoulders told of their various discoveries: of fruits fallen from trees, of seeds from sacks being conveyed to the marketplace, of new nesting grounds on the other side of the Eastern Sea. One nighthawk spoke proudly of her young eyas taking flight for the first time, and another pronounced the same only her eyas flew longer and higher than the first hawk's had done. Some spoke of worms billowing and burrowing out from the ground during the morning rains, some spoke of their good fortune to beat the owls at catching mice, and while this was idle raillery to the birds, it was all felicity to Khantara, whose only wish for the remainder of the evening was to be quiet and indulgent.

His quietude, however, was suddenly broken; he came to the end of the lane whereupon he observed the lights in the windows of a small home. Though the house had always been at the end of the path, he had never noticed it before; his walks were usually taken well past gloaming, once all the business and animation in the markets had done and all fires within the homes had gone out. Now, however, the house at the end of the lane with its want of splendor, its gabled yard, its unadorned windows, its cheerlessness, beckoned his notice. It was a pitiable home, one quite hidden away from the rest of the human settlement, separated by a sanded walkway and a line of weeping ferns.

The situation and consequence of the house, however, had not disturbed Khantara so much as the commotion within it had done. A few strident shouts from a male voice rang out, and in another moment, the front door to the house was thrown open and out stormed a furious and ranting Thellisian man. He thundered down the sanded walkway leading toward the more lively part of the settlement, but was stopped by someone emerging from the home. A woman appeared in the doorway, terrified and anxious, her shoulders tense and her hands in a pleading posture as though begging the man not to leave. She said a few inaudible words and hastened to the edge of the yard to detain him further.

Khantara watched them speak to one another from his place in the shadows and studied their apparent disparities while they were engaged in strained conversation. Where the man was short and robust, the woman was tall and frail, and where he was stout and well-dressed, less could be said for her. The woman's dress was unremarkable and faded, her complexion pastel, and her person saddened and distressed. A few terse and unkind phrases passed from the man to the woman: he would be going out, he would be enjoying his time at the tavern and inn, and he would give her no answer of when he should be expected to return when asked. He turned to leave, but the woman would convince him to stay: she had a shy look about her, offered him a warm meal and a promise of something more later in the evening, but her desperate attempt did not answer. The man seemed appalled and angered by her offer. He scoffed in disdain, turned his back, and continued toward town, leaving the woman standing at the edge of the yard with little more than her wounded pride and bare feet to support her dampened spirits. For a moment, she seemed as though she might call out to him, but her mortification had silenced her. She appeared despondent at the man's departure despite the cruelty with which she had been treated. She regarded the lights of town in the distance and sighed, seemingly more disappointed in herself for failing to endear him than she was at being publically harangued. She turned toward the house but could not continue; she was too disconsolate to reenter the empty and somber home. Her shoulders wilted, her full lips pouted and quivered, and with a mortified sigh, she wept into her hand.

Khantara could bear the sight of the woman standing before the dreadful home no longer. He must try to assist and console her, if she would accept his company, but as he separated from the shadows and walked toward her, he was stopped by the sight of a strange brand on the side of her neck. The Thellisian symbol for 'marked' was burned into her flesh, and though it could not answer for the exchange he had just witnessed, it could explain her bare feet and poor dress. He was aware of Thellisian slaves and thought her to be one, but her missing restraints, upright figure and elegant hands told him otherwise. He found, however, other features to excite his curiosity: a braid of thick hair so long as to sweep the backs of her thighs was his chief delight; blue-green eyes and a tinge of colour in her cheeks were his other concerns. He made a slow approach as she wiped her tears, and he bowed to her to gain her attention and convey his gentle civility.

In between her quiet sobs, the woman felt herself being overcome by a shadow. She looked up to discover an immense creature standing before her and inclining his head in her direction. She looked about her to see if there was someone behind her who deserved such propriety, but there was no one in the vicinity excepting herself and the giant. Astonished by such gallantry, she greeted him with the same forthcoming gesture and quickly dispatched all of her remaining tears. *A Haanta*, she thought, *here. But what can he want with me?* was the question that plagued her for some minutes when the giant remained in silence. She blushed first in a glow of animation to welcome so immense, so unspoken and so unexpected a creature, but all her happiness soon became embarrassment; he must have overheard her conversation and had now come to question the conflict. She lowered her head, touched the brand on her neck, and waited for a reproof with downcast eyes, but no such reproof came; he remarked her with a thoughtful expression and said nothing. She thought perhaps that Haanta custom called for her to speak first, though she knew not what was proprietous to say. She fidgeted with her hands, shifted in place, and began with, "Have you lost your way, sir?" in an expectant tone, hoping that the giant could understand the Thellisian language.

Khantara made a momentary smile and his eyes were aglow to see her features brighten. "No," was his soft answer.

The woman stepped back, struck by the resonation of his low voice. *He spoke to her:* the creature of majesty, the dark mountain cloaked in shadow with nighthawks adorning his shoulders spoke to *her*. Her breath quickened, her mouth curled into a wider smile, her heart filled with the warmth of wonder, but soon fancies of her own inadequacy returned. He could not be here for her, for who was she but a marked woman? He must be here for someone else. His presence was too good of a mistake, and though she wished that he were here on her account by some means of providential intervention, she would not deceive herself only to be disappointed. "Have you come here on your way to town?" she said in a small voice. "If you are uncertain of the way there, I can show you, sir. But I can only lead you as far as the marketplace."

Khantara only smiled.

Presently she added, "I'm not permitted to go to town, but I can point out the way from the edge of the markets if you need a guide."

The giant did not answer. He was observing her uneasy motions, long swaying braid, thin figure and scarred neck. He stepped closer to her to judge her reaction, and to his contentment, she did not retract from him. He hummed in deliberation and narrowed his gaze.

After some minutes of mutual silence, she began to feel as though she had stepped out of her place and thus began to excuse herself. "I don't mean to disturb you if you were only meaning to pass by, sir. I apologize for my forwardness." She lowered her eyes. "It was wrong of me to assume that you would want my help." She smiled and made a timorous laugh. "I often mistake people addressing me for their wanting my company."

Khantara observed her trembling hands. "You have called me 'sir'," he said, turning the subject. "Is this a title your people give to others?"

Her knees weakened at the continual sound of his voice. "It's a respectful title for a man used in place of a person's name." She turned her head and pointed to her brand. "I'm one of the Marked. I'm not permitted to call anyone by name unless given permission."

Khantara's brow bent in anguish to see such a delicate complexion ruined. "What are you called?" he said, gesturing toward her.

She placed a hand on her breast. "My name, sir?"

The giant hummed and nodded.

"Anelta is my name, sir."

"And your mate calls you by this title?"

Anelta glanced toward town. "He does," said Anelta in a pained voice.

"And does this designation have meaning?"

She paused to consider and then said, "It might, but I cannot answer you, sir. I think it could be Old Thellisian for something, but I wasn't permitted to attend the Academy so I was never able to learn."

Khantara looked into the windows of the home behind her and saw no movement other than the flickering light of a dying fire within. "Your mate leaves you alone for the evening?" he said in mild condemnation.

Anelta looked away, and said with half a sigh, "He comes and goes, as he likes."

"And you do the same?"

"No, sir. The Marked aren't allowed to go into town." He seemed to be growing concerned for her, and to reassure him, she added, "But I can go to the Church and to the marketplace, which is more than what I was allowed when living at the shelter."

"Hmm," was the giant's rumbling reply. He had heard of Thellis' self-oppression but had never conceived of its going this far. For a nation to refuse education to their own was to diminish the value of its people, and Khantara could not agree with the woman's exclusion despite knowing little of her. To keep one so eager as ignorant, regardless of situation and consequence in society, was an attestation of Thellis' unbidden malice. He could only hope the rest of the mainland did not maintain such a practice.

When the giant said nothing more, Anelta began to worry that she had misspoken or spoken too much. She was grateful for his attention and his making her happy again, but now he must go lest she begin to wish him to stay longer than was advisable. "Well, thank you for your conversation, sir," she said with a bow.

This was a strange appreciation. He eyed her with misgiving and would enquire further if to sate his own curiosity then to also make her remain longer with him. "Are others prohibited from speaking to you?"

"Sometimes," she shrugged. "It depends upon the person's rank in society. Normally I cannot speak to anyone unless approached first." And then, with a smile and a blush, "It's kind of you to stay so long, sir."

"You may call me by my Amghari designation of Khantara," the giant purred, inclining his head to accompany the formal introduction.

"Khantara," Anelta softly repeated. "Is this what your people call you?"

"Some do. Many call me Odaibha."

"Is this a special rank?"

"My rank is Den Amhadhri," the giant tenderly corrected her. "Odaibha is a term used for one who is skilled in many things."

"Oh," Anelta said, feeling a sense of awe prevail her. "Which title is acceptable for subordinates to use? I would feel strange to call you by name if you have other more respected titles I should be using."

"You may use whatever title you wish," he said smilingly. "Has your mate given you an honourable title?"

Anelta's cheeks crimsoned in shame. "I don't think some of the words he has called me are honourable."

Khantara gathered her meaning and regarded her with utmost consideration. "You are alone often?"

"He enjoys the food and music of the inns and the company of the women there," she said, excusing his conduct rather than answering for herself. "He comes back once every few days."

Such inattention was insufferable, and Khantara wondered at how this behavior was permitted to endure. Surely her mate must be aware of her inability to venture to town, and though the marketplace and Church was allowable, how could she be expected to be alone for days together? Should there be no food left or should something happen to their home, she should be stranded with no one to assist her. She did not seem incapable by any means, regardless of what the brand on her neck communicated, but being so confined and in such a manner was an inconceivable wrong. Khantara felt for her misfortune, for if she had a Haanta mate, this situation would never have occurred: Haanta who made such a promise to one so carefully selected would not permit such neglect. Khantara now understood this abandonment, and in his growing dislike for her way of living, he was moved to ask, "Your mate does not provide for you?"

"He does," she said, looking nervously about. "I have a home away from the shelter, which is more than most of the Marked receive. I have food when he is here. I was even allowed to purchase food for myself until recently, but I purchased a few items at the marketplace without asking if I could. I like to try different things just to see what I can make, and sometimes it gets the better of me."

"It is natural that you would wish to challenge yourself," Khantara said, acquitting her of any culpable feelings she might yet have.

"But," she added, shrinking her voice, "he said I should have consulted him first. He was angry with me for buying items that he didn't ask me to bring home." Her cheeks flushed and she raised her hand to her brow. "I don't think he will be happy with me again for some time," she said in a timorous hush, and then chiding herself, "I should have asked for permission first."

"Is this why he refused you?"

A gasp, a blush, and all her fears were realized: he *had* seen their exchange. "Well—" she muttered, but her speech was checked by her humiliation. She looked at her feet and bit her lower lip. "I don't think . . . That is—I mean to say—I could hardly be considered appealing, I think."

"Your mate would not choose you if he did not believe you to be inviting," Khantara hoped.

"I wish I could look better than I do. I'm not so pretty as he would like."

Khantara eyed her with grim confusion. "Your mate has told you this?"

"A few times." Anelta wished to excuse herself here, but she could not. She believed that if she dressed in a certain manner, walked a certain way, and followed the example of those she had seen about the markets that she might be forgiven all her faults, but as she had no means of improvement, she could only lament and reproach herself. "I don't really know how women should act or how they should look in the way that men like," she murmured. "I always wanted to learn how to make myself look more like the women in town, but no one ever showed me. I have tried a few times on my own, but I have seen what he prefers and I don't think I could compare. I have asked some of the other Marked in the marketplace but they don't know either."

"You are permitted to learn from no one else other than your own?"

"No," Anelta said, sensing the giant's censure. "Once, when my husband was away, I tried to find some work, one of the small jobs given to the Marked who are more capable, just so that I might learn a trade, but I couldn't read the charge I was given and I was turned away."

"You cannot read or write your own language?" Khantara could not abide such a notion: the ignorant forced to glean what morsels of knowledge they could from their superiors only to tell one another of what the other had learned was a deplorable arrangement, and though he did not mean to show his indignation, he felt he could not hide it from her.

"I want to learn, sir," Anelta pleaded. "I remember a few characters from when I was very young. I tried to teach myself to read a few times, but my husband caught me looking at his books one day and he wasn't pleased. He told me not to touch his things ever again." It seemed to her that the more she spoke, the more besieged the giant became. She thought she had said something wrong and thought now would be a prudent time to remove from his company before any more harm could be done. "I'm sorry. I'm detaining you when I should be on my way to the Church."

Khantara moved in her path to impede her from leaving. "There is a service this evening you must attend?"

"The Marked aren't allowed inside for services, but sometimes the Church gives out donations to those who need food. It's not easy to convince them in my case. They say that help is meant for those who don't have relations or a home, but sometimes the Sisters are kind to me and give me what is left of their meal."

"You have nothing to eat while your mate is away?"

Anelta lowered her eyes and was silent.

Khantara paused and regarded the woman with a most dreadful countenance. "Your mate does not willingly share what is his with you?"

She wished to give an assenting reply, but his look told her that no matter what answer she could deliver, he had formed his own opinions on the subject.

While Anelta was struck with the horror of having offended the giant by her candor, Khantara had resolved that caring for so forthcoming and deprived a woman would be his object until nightfall required him to return to his people. The commemoration made in his honour could wait where there was kindness to be done, and instead of returning to the celebration and rejoining his commanders, he sat beside one of the weeping ferns, gathered his long unkempt locks into his lap, and bid Anelta to attend him. He motioned for her to take the space beside him, but she seemed hesitant to obey. He reached into his Dhanna to produce Phoraas, and he held the wrapped meal toward her to remake the invitation.

"Come," he said with firm benevolence. "Share with me."

And come she did.

She sat beside the giant and watched him intently as he opened the odd meal, peeling back the dried leaves on the surface to reveal a mix of grains and herbs billowing with steam. He used the leaves to divide the meal in half and gave her the larger of the two portions with the readiest compassion.

The Compassion of a Mountain

hough she had no notion of what she was being given, Anelta said all the profuse and quiet thanks necessary for so generous a meal. She spied, she scrutinized, she inhaled, she marveled, and the wrawling sounds of her stomach conveyed that she was prepared to devour her meal, but her own sense of duty to what was owed the charitable giant compelled her to wait until after the giant had eaten first. She, however, was given that honour: with a nod and a pleasant smile, she was bid to begin. She did so, somewhat hesitatingly, and had not even swallowed the first mouthful when she was overcome by the warmth and satisfaction the strange food accorded. Her shivering abated, her worrying cogitations ceased, but after her initial gratitude had done with her, she had yet more to suffer: the verity of someone caring for her and assisting her besieged her, rousing sentiments so pleasantly distressing that she was moved to tears. She ate with shaking hands and quiet sobs, doing her utmost to screen her reddening eyes from her benefactor and failing miserably.

Khantara now understood the extent of her privations: her condition had not been one of recent neglect, but it had been one of prolonged and purposeful inattention. He grieved for her, watching her lick the steamed grains from her fingers while using her arm to wipe the tears from her face. This was a sorrowful scene for him to witness, but it was one that began to alter his considerations on conquering Thellis. He wondered now if such cruelty was prevalent everywhere in the enemy nation, and if it was, he wondered that more Thellisians should not have been willing to join his people if only to escape the horrors of neglect and privation.

"Is this a special meal for your people?" Anelta asked after being certain to eat every grain stuck to the dried leaves.

"It is called Phoraas, and it is made for our warriors." Khantara observed how much she had eaten in so little time and smilingly said, "You will not be hungry for some time."

She still felt hungry, however, though less so than she had before. "Won't I?"

Khantara shook his head. "The amount you have eaten is what one of our warriors is meant to eat in a day."

"Then I should have saved some," Anelta lamented.

"No, you must have more."

Khantara had eaten so little of his portion that there was more than enough to give Anelta another significant helping. He offered all that was in his hands to her, but the birds adorning his shoulders felt differently toward his generosity. They would have some of his meal regardless of the starving woman; their eager twitters told him so, but his silent entreaties and explanations of Anelta's difficulty made them happy with a few grains to furnish their beaks.

Anelta, however, could not accept such an offering; this was far too much kindness for one so meager in consequence, but her hunger soon overcame her validation, and after some gentle entreaties on the giant's side, she found herself able to accept. She ate at a more measured pace with the hopes that her hunger should lessen the more time she left between bites, but while she was occupied with reminding herself not to betray how hungry she was by eating with such rapidity, she had allowed something else to happen: her arm had accidentally brushed against the giant's. For an instant, she felt his warmth and the strength of his immense arm hidden beneath a silken cloth. She blushed, ashamed more for enjoying the feeling than she was of her unintentional conduct, and moved slightly away that he might not notice her embarrassment. He had noticed, however: between her small mouthfuls of grain, she glanced in his direction to catch any hint of his discernment, and she was mortified to discover him smiling down at her. He was passing intermittent looks toward her and then toward where she had touched him. She turned from him, wanting to look back again and wanting not to look all at once, and acknowledged that though she could conceal the flush in her features, she could not hide it in the tips of her ears or along the nape of her neck.

Though she might pretend that the gentle connection did not occur, Khantara could not but acknowledge and approve it. While she was otherwise engaged, he shifted closer to her to reclaim his proximity with the aspiration that she should be so careless again. He wished for her to feel comfortable around him, and if she needed to glean warmth from him that she would, but he must recognize that her society was not his and she had probably not been used to such amiable interest. For so slender a touch to make her so ashamed supplied him with proof of her segregation. He found her indignity endearing and said nothing of the incident though he might wish to speak of it if only to have her in such an animation of spirits until his leave.

Together they remained until the sun vanished over the horizon. The darkening of the skies and coming of the luminaries meant that the giant must part from the woman and return to his people for the end of the ceremony made in his honour. He stood first and offered his hand to her to assist her to her feet, but she had been too quick in rising and too eager to see him off that he missed the opportunity for courteous gestures.

She bowed to him and thanked him once more, and before he could answer the gesture, she said in a shy voice, "I hope that we will meet again, sir."

"Khantara," he kindly reminded her, bowing low.

She repeated his name in an inaudible whisper as though she were speaking the title in confidence, secreting it away for her own private enjoyment. The more she iterated the designation, the more partial to it she became: she had been permitted to call him by name, and not merely an indication of rank as Den Amhadhri or Odaibha might have been, but a name she could use that would not signify her lowness in comparison. It was such a gift, a name to say over and over without fear of admonishment, and she smiled at his parting with all the exuberance such a wondrous moment could afford.

Khantara, however, was not granted the same happiness when he turned to leave Anelta. In stepping away from the house and toward the lane leading to the Haanta settlement, he felt a pang of instant regret: regret for leaving her in so terrible a place, regret for not having more food to give her at present; for leaving her with no one to speak to or anyone to regard her, and the only manner in which he could quit the woman and the small unseemly home was to vow to revisit on the morrow with more to give than just his company. He did not tell her of his intended return, for he wished to see more of what she endured while he was not present in order to understand the full extent of her situation. Further intercourse with her mate, an interaction with another Marked, or even watching her alone would suffice. He inclined his head, forced a smile, and passed down the darkened lane with the birds on his shoulders all alive with excitement while his mind was employed with other concerns.

Anelta watched the mountainous shadow shamble away from her in happy agitation. She had some fears that she had little to offer the giant in the ways of conversation and hospitality due to the state of the home in which she was impelled to live, and due to her inability to convey more than what she felt, but never had she considered herself so honoured than to have spent above an hour in the giant's shadow. To have pressed his arm, to have shared his meal, and to have spoken to him without the fear of punishment was all felicity to her. She hoped, with all that was in her power, that he would come again, and whether his coming was tomorrow or a season hence, it made little difference. She reckoned that his coming at all was worth any wait, and to say the name of Khantara while under his guard once more was more rapture than she could bear. Though she could no longer see his form passing away down the lane, she heard the birds on his shoulders and the trees bustle with a ripple of chirps to mark his path. She wondered why the birds seemed to answer and flock to him, and in her blind curiosity, she took a step forward as though to follow him. His nature, his person, his air had attracted her. Who were his people and how did they live were questions she began to ask herself. Were they all as generous and as tender as he seemed to be, or was he the exception? Who was he to come to her in such a manner and treat her with such equality? Was he someone who was accustomed to such charity of feeling and openhandedness, or was he one of the great conquerors come to destroy their nation through munificence and promises of liberation? Too great a mistake it was that he should have come to her, and Anelta stood at the edge of yard beside the weeping ferns blessing her good fortune, praising whatever powers were at fault for sending her someone who could abide her discourse and who seemed so much in want of her conversancy.

A Home for a Conqueror

With a heavy heart did Khantara return to the Haanta settlement. The first faint and now increasing music of the celebration, the twittering and chattering of the birds, the distant gaiety and mirth of his people could do nothing to secure his happiness. He admired the curiosity of the nighthawks on his shoulders as to why his thoughts remained around a single woman when the digging up of worms must be far more interesting to him, and smiled once or twice when realizing that they were only trying to cheer him. He felt some moments of sanguine warmth when observing his people gather into the ceremonial grounds for the ending festivities, but his contentment could not last long when he had left one so dejected and deprived behind him. He wished now that he could bring her to the settlement at least until her mate should return. This gesture would have secured his partial ease, but it would have ended upon having to give her away again. To return her to such a home and force her to live in such a manner was an unbearable yet indelible distress, and the only hope Khantara had for renewing his joy was in seeing his three Amhadhri.

He was fortunate to find one of them standing outside the celebration grounds. He had thought that the commander should prefer employing himself in the barracks or in the training yard as he had been used to do during the celebrations on the islands, but instead the Amhadhri of immense stature, obsidian skin and silent conviction was standing at the end of the lane and seemed to be looking for his master's return.

The Amhadhri's eyes flared in quiet elation when seeing Khantara appear from the shadows. "Odaibha," he said, bowing stiffly and low.

Khantara inclined his head and observed the look of severe disquiet in his commander's countenance. "I am well, Mhardhosa," he assured him.

Mhardhosa made a curt nod, but his severity remained. He knew he had his master's confidence, as did the other Amhadhri, but as his master had seemed so adamant to be alone, he made no question as to where he went or what he saw.

Khantara gave his Amhadhri a caring look, and then glancing toward the celebration said, "Are your brothers within?"

"Bhaaldhena is watching the dance, and Jhiaanta is apologizing to the Mhojhudenri," said Mhardhosa in a hurried and pained voice. An immense dark grey hand was placed upon his shoulder and he remarked it with an appeased sigh.

Upon hearing Mhardhosa's evening report, Khantara shook his head. "He cannot resist and he must always have Jhiaanta excuse his conduct," was his smiling grievance. "Did he leave some Abharaas for others?"

Mhardhosa looked to the side. "Some."

"Hmm. I will speak with him."

Mhardhosa would have refuted his Odaibha's speeches doing any good, but he checked himself and remained silent, bowing to his master as he passed into the celebration and wondering whether Jhiaanta had not scolded their brother already.

There was an immediate uproar when Khantara entered the commemoration, one so exuberant and strident as to make it seem as though he had not been present at the festival's inception. The dancers came to saunter about him, the music changed from melodious beats to happy trills, and every celebrant gathered to him to greet him with cordial bows and to solicit him to accept their commendations. His

people's enthusiasm and delight at his attendance added to his, and in their teeming and pleasant company, Khantara found his solace. He observed Jhiaanta and Bhaaldhena standing near the tables, the former bowing to the provisioner in apology and latter exhibiting his overwhelming might to a flock of young passing women. The giant's unmistakable presence and prolonged look in their direction soon caught their awareness, and both of them bowed to their master from their places, each of them wanting to approach but unable to do so with so many about him, each of them with equally guilty and reproachful looks for the other. Khantara half-smiled to himself, his heart warmed by Jhiaanta and Bhaaldhena's behaviour, for though he may have wished that they would act with more prudence during public observances—but perhaps with less stern reservation than that of their brother Mhardhosa—he could not have been more pleased to see them at their usual larks. Bhaaldhena playful and boastful, Jhiaanta fretful and repentant, and seeing them act toward one another with the same opposing natures as they had done when they were mere Mivaari was all Khantara's boundless exhilaration.

He gave all his attention to the expectant crowds bustling about him, answering their questions and treating their tributes of flowers for his hand with the kindest esteem, until a stonecutter approached the giant with a bow and a request to come with him to the entrance of the celebration. Khantara obliged the invitation and begged his leave, avowing to return soon, and nodded to Jhiaanta and Bhaaldhena for them to join him. They leapt to him, impeding the crowds of people from following him with their immense forms, and when they assembled together at the entrance to the celebration grounds, Mhardhosa joined the party, taking his place between his two brothers as Khantara and the stonecutter spoke.

"*Kodhanaas*, Den Amhadhri," said the stonecutter with a bow to Khantara. "I am pleased to tell you that your home is prepared." The stonecutter seemed very well pleased with himself and was surprised that his beneficiary seemed less so.

The gesture was well-meant, but where it had every good intention behind it, it could not be accepted without some aggrievement on Khantara's side. He looked away and sighed. "Vhasthusa," he thrummed, "I am honoured to be considered before others for residency, but our people need a temple and shelter more than a Den Amhadhri needs a home."

Vhasthusa looked to the three commanders for their assessment, but none of them would contend their master's ruling. "It was the Themari's request, and it was one I was more than honoured to fulfill," said the stonecutter, hoping the explanation would mean his recipient's gratitude, but it did not; it could not when there were so many others yet waiting for their homes to be built and when the whole of the collective was waiting for their temple to be finished.

"I will have to speak to our Themari," Khantara said disappointedly. "You have my thanks, Vhasthusa."

They bowed to one another, but it was a bow of solemn appreciation: Khantara could not consent to being put before others when he could very well care for himself, and the stonecutter was unused to receive such somber thanks for such excellent work.

Feeling slighted, the stonecutter proclaimed, "I have shown your Amhadhri where your residence is situated. They may take you to it," and left Khantara's presence.

There was no manner in which to pay compliment without paying insult in this situation: were Khantara to be overjoyed that his home were finished before others in the Haanta settlement, it would betray him as complacent and prideful, but were he to be livid at such a prospect, it would show an ingratitude that was undue. He must offend somebody a little to settle the matter in a peaceful quarter, and he would rather have the affront given to the Themari for requesting such an impropriety than with anyone else involved. Khantara was sorry to have made the stonecutter feel undervalued, but he would choose one person to feel so rather than the entire Haanta collective to feel irrelevant. He would make a more comprehensible thanks to the stonecutter after having visited the house to close and rectify the business, but now the Themari must be reproached. Khantara therefore excused himself from his Amhadhri to screen them from the disapprobation he must unfortunately relay and went to where the Themari stood near the musician's pavilion.

One disenchanted look from Khantara told the Themari of his vast displeasure, and the giant required no words to convey his sentiments on the Themari's judgment. The Themari, however, had taken it a matter of course that their beloved conqueror should given his home before anyone else should be given theirs. New habitations were being carved and hollowed out by the day, and as most of the Haanta collective were already secured, it was only a matter of a week before everyone should be accommodated, but this would not do for Khantara. Whether it be a few days, a week or an hour, he would see everyone indulged before himself. He was silent through the Themari's fumbling speech, and when the priest had done, Khantara's final word was, "Our Mivaari sleep in an unfinished temple and you would give *me* a home? You would give a home to one who does not need rest before you would have our Mivaari, our legacy, accommodated?" And it was said with such finality and such pointedness as to make the Themari silent on the subject forever. He could only be rueful, and Khantara would not silence his apologies. "Ask for Khostaas from our people," Khantara said with firmness. "They are the ones who must suffer because of your decision."

The Themari agreed that he would and begged for Khantara's forgiveness.

"I will attend the Mivaari in the morning," he said, turning to leave, "and I will have the Amhadhri assist those who are working on the temple." He was not to be argued with, and when he returned to his Amhadhri, the Themari exhaled and said praises for Khantara's kindly and magnanimous character. Were he of a more ambitious and vindictive nature, he should have no scruple in sending word of the misjudgment to the high priest on Mhavhaledhran, and to Khantara's leniency and tranquility, the Themari was eternally beholden.

Khantara was well composed by the time he returned to his commanders, but though he was now in his indulgent humour once more, he kept a stern look for Bhaaldhena who, though well-meaning and merely wishing to quell some of his inexhaustible hunger, had eaten the chief of the Abharaas at the celebration. It was true that there was ever more to be put out upon the tables, but that a further abundance should have been brought for one who was meant to be practicing moderacy was not acceptable form. He raised his brow and said in a tone of mild castigation, "Bhaaldhena."

Bhaaldhena's taupe-coloured skin darkened. "Khostaas, Odaibha," he quietly begged, seeming ashamed of himself but hardly repentant; his full stomach and suppressed appetite made him far too contended for remorse.

Khantara sighed, but it was a sigh more of relief than of frustration. Though ever younger than himself, his commanders were old enough now that their behaviour could not be changed, and in this instance, he must confess it gave him a certain appeasement to think that Bhaaldhena should suppress his inbred hunger in this manner than in a more deleterious one. When he considered this, he made a conscious look to Mhardhosa, whose severe countenance was beginning to cringe in agony as the music of the celebration and the commotion of its attendants grew louder with the closing of the festivities.

Jhiaanta was also sensible of Mhardhosa's pained looks. "May we lead you to your home, Odaibha?" he suggested, glancing significantly at his agonized brother.

"You may," Khantara replied, motioning for his commanders to move away from the celebration grounds. "First, I must thank our people and then we will go."

They moved far enough away that Mhardhosa's comfort could be tolerably secured and waited for their master to return, but not two minutes had passed when Jhiaanta suddenly elbowed Bhaaldhena in the ribs and said, "I told you he would not be pleased," in a begrudging tone.

"No," said Bhaaldhena, mockingly patting his little brother on the head, "but I ate well, and he will forgive me by tomorrow."

Jhiaanta, enough agitated by his brother's conduct, had his patience tried by his dismissive sentiments. He forcibly pushed the large hand on his head away and was about to continue his remonstrance when the same hand returned to him to cover his mouth.

The fight, playful on Bhaaldhena's account and struggling on Jhiaanta's, was over as soon as it had begun. One vicious look from Mhardhosa had decided it: neither would win, and if the severe Amhadhri should have to apply his abilities upon them to make them still, he would. They were far enough away from the celebration to have his concentration restored, but his ruthless rage could be exercised at any time he so wished.

The thought of this occurred to the two squabbling Amhadhri and each of them responded accordingly: Jhiaanta traded places with Bhaaldhena to use him as a shield, and Bhaaldhena placed his hands on the handle of his weapons and made a broad grin. Their readiness, however, soon proved needless: Khantara was already returning from the celebration and Bhaaldhena's expectation of a most interesting battle was lost.

With the Haanta collective thanked for their attention and the prospect of a spending the remainder of the night in silence within an isolated home pending, Khantara allowed his Amhadhri to guide him away from the celebration grounds. A few moments spent listening to the stridulations of crickets and chirrups of night wrens and Khantara felt once more as he should: serene, silent, observant and in the company of those most precious to him. Watching his three commanders walk before him engaged in quiet discourse in the cool of the evening granted him the feelings he had before the war with Thellis had begun: they were yet on Mhavhaledhran, he was yet their teacher, they were still young and all of them taking a walk along the shore together with only the copses of trees, grey sands, and the line of the horizon to remark. There were similar prospects on the mainland, but the shore was north in this part of the mainland and the only portion permitted to traverse was near the docks. The remainder of the coastline was part of the Thellisian settlement; they could walk there, with their intimidating heights and impressive strengths to recommend their safety on such a journey, but to have the Thellisians fear them any more than they already did was an injudicious venture.

Discussion of what was to be done for the barracks at sunrise ended Khantara's internalizations. He told them that they were to accompany him to the temple to remedy the Themari's error in judgment and no more on the subject was said. Though Bhaaldhena may have wished to visit the weaponsmakers to inquire about furnishing the racks in the barracks for coming warriors and Jhiaanta may have wanted to set up his targets, Mhardhosa would have done nothing else then remain more in his master's company if he could; going to the temple with him should be a blessing to his disconcerted mind. It was difficult enough for him to find his peace on the islands, and in coming to a new land with so many new sounds to endure and so much disdain toward their people to brook, Mhardhosa was in desperate need of his dependant and saviour. He relished being in his shadow wherever it may have fallen, and though he must train and spend much of his time in quieting rumination to achieve any semblance of composure, he found more comfort in sidling his master than any in meditation or ritual.

A few moments of walking along the main road of the Haanta settlement and they came to the house. It was screened from the moonlight by the overhang of the large willow boughs beside it, but it was lit enough from the fires along the road that Khantara was able to judge its make. The small residence of hollowed out and carved sandstone, ornamented by his chirping friends and etched with the phrases of the Haanta ordinances, stood in a small nook hidden by the few mills and working accoutrements beside it. Its position marked the halfway point between the Haanta settlement and the barracks, and though it was a short distance to each by any means, it was thought that this should be the perfect situation for one who shared duties of an Odaibha and a Den Amhadhri: the distance to the temple was the distance to the training yard. Khantara made a hum of approval for its placing and exterior, but what would be within? His Amhadhri parted from his path and urged him to look into his new home, and there he found all the simplicity and quietness he could have desired: there was a small living area with a few of the pelts he had been awarded for his prowess at Endaraas, the hunting of hangaara cats, draped across the ground; there was another small room with a stone bed covered with a few more pelts; and behind that a small area for washing. It was faultless in its execution, wholly tasteful and modest in every respect. When Khantara turned toward the entrance to ask his Amhadhri what they thought of the home, he was surprised to find them kneeling to him and Jhiaanta the foremost before them with his hand outstretched.

"Please, Odaibha," Jhiaanta said, lowering his head and holding something out to him. "You would honour us by accepting our gift."

In Jhiaanta's hand was a golden censer carved in the shape of the Kai Linaa, the Haanta life giver, with a cistern in her arms. He held it up for his master to take and said thanks for allowing them into his most venerated home. They stood when the gift was accepted, but Jhiaanta could not help but notice that his master seemed forlorn, not from any dissatisfaction with the residence or their tribute but rather from a remembrance he could not obviate.

"Are you not pleased, Odaibha?" said Jhiaanta gently.

Khantara recollected himself and placed his hand on Jhiaanta's shoulder. "There is little that displeases me, Jhiaanta," he softly reminded him." The notion that had so discomposed him rushed on him when he beheld the image of the Kai Linaa. He thought of the wealth and consequence of his people, the liberality and felicity abound, but when he saw the Haanta life giver in his hand, made of gold and carved with the most careful execution, he was compelled to think of Anelta. He had left her there in a home of wretchedness and misery, and he was now enjoying a residence of what seemed like sumptuousness in comparison. Inscribed walls, trappings along the ground, his companions adorning the flat roof, blooming willows beside his window, his Amhadhri to share in his joy: all of it was so joyous to him and yet made evil by considering the despondency and paucity of others. He remained silent for some time, remarking the gift with an air of gravity and melancholy.

"Odaibha?" asked Bhaaldhena, hoping to awaken his master.

Khantara could not wish Anelta's situation unseen, for to do so would render her an unimportant discovery. He did, however, wish to be rid of the aching sensation in his chest and the ill feeling in his stomach. "I do not approve this conquering of nations," he said in a slow drone, placing the gift on the small stone table beside the open window. "However, if we conquer them only to end their cruel practices, I will be greatly consoled."

The three Amhadhri looked at one another and surmised that their master had seen something along his walk to distress him.

"May I ask what you witnessed, Odaibha?" said Bhaaldhena.

Khantara paused to consider and then said, "Those of Thellis mark and enslave their own people. They forbid them from learning and place them in homes with no one to care for their needs."

"Why would they do this, Odaibha?" asked Jhiaanta.

The question could not be answered, and with a shake of the head and a downcast eye, Khantara said, "I do not know why a nation so great would willingly subjugate and demean its people."

"Are those who are marked ill in any way?"

"The one I met was not. She seemed more than able . . ." but Khantara surrendered to thoughts of Anelta and stopped here. The subject was too painful to be revived and he closed their conversation with, "We must remember to always treat others with kindness and never harm those who have no means of defense."

The Amhadhri understood the sentiment that had inspired the repetition of their earliest lesson and in unison promised to obey his command. They thought it advisable now to leave their master to the comfort that solitude could merit and left with equal bows and avowals of joining him in the morning. Upon quitting the home, however, Jhiaanta turned back in time to see his master conversing with a few of the small creatures that had found their way to his window. He observed how even his usual comforts afforded him little reprieve from his sorrows, and he thought to turn back and keep his master company when his brothers called him away to practice their Kaatas till sunrise. He felt his heart wrench as he left his master, and he could only hope that Khantara would be easy again by the time they should return.

Now alone and every duty to his people and Amhadhri fulfilled, Khantara was at liberty to sit on the ground of his new home and meditate over the most engaging day. It had been a morning of exertion, an evening of education and a night of intolerable indecency. The home, however, would be his consolation until morning. There he could reflect and ponder as he ought to do to make sense of Anelta's situation. He removed his Dhanna and his axe from his back and sat on the hangaara pelt in the center of the main room. He folded his muscular legs over one another, rubbed his feet, his soles burned black and skin rough from his arduous training, and flexed his gargantuan arms and back in preparation for his evening practice of Haakhas. The Haanta observance of deep rumination always provided him with the peace he sought, but after a few moments of whispering the passages, his meditations soon bore a different character. There was confusion and anxiety when he would have stillness; too many questions attacked his mind: why was she seen as a slave if she had a mate, why was her mate permitted to leave her, why was she left with no means of sustenance or comfort were all beleaguering queries that could not be silenced. He had already resolved to visit her on the morrow, but his conscience could not allow him to do it later than was necessary. Another evening visit would not do for him; he must go earlier, he must go before she would become too hungry and be forced to travel alone in quest of nourishment, he must—but he stopped himself here, opening his eyes and exhaling with great aggravation. Although he had his duties in the temple at sunrise and his duties at the barracks in the afternoon, he would find time between his obligations if not to assist her than to quell his own discomforts on the woman's account.

Khantara sat in silent meditation for the rest of the evening and only opened his black and yellow eyes once to remark the shaft of moonlight pervading the open window, casting shadows of birds nesting on the sill along the stone ground.

The Haanta Settlement

ot a few hours had passed and Khantara had deemed himself done with his daily rest. Thoughts of the woman, though less frequent, still reigned in his mind, and though it pained him to think of her situation, he found a certain comfort in thinking of her person. There was an innocence about her, rather than an ignorance, which he liked. She was eager and a novelty, ready to learn and wanting to try. If only he were her Odaibha and if only he could teach her as he did all the Mivaari of the Haanta settlement, but as he considered this and made his gentle genuflections to rock him out of his meditative state, he knew that teaching the Haanta way of life to those who did not ask was ill-advised. She would have to request to be taught by him if any knowledge was to be passed between them. She would make a most excellent student and he should revel in teaching her. An inquisitive look, a question, a hint was all he should need to tell her what he had learned in his hundred years, and at the very least to teach her to read and write her own language if not his people's native tongue. He opened his eyes, stood slowly from his place, and began saying his morning Haakhas while stretching his massive form. He went to the washing area tucked away behind the bedchamber and began washing his feet, hands and face while finishing the repetition of the Haanta scriptures. As he dried himself with the cloth beside the wooden basin, he said a few words of silent thanks for his new home, one that had offered him much of the peace he had been so desirous of attaining.

The skies were yet dark, but the stars were beginning to fade with the coming of morning. Sunrise would be in an hour hence, and he resolved to employ his time looking in' on the barracks and training yard before he must go to the temple with his Amhadhri and visit his youngest students. He placed his axe at his back, donned his Dhanna and left his residence in a more blithesome humour than when he had entered it the night before.

The instant Khantara began to walk the short path to the barracks he was attacked by swarms of wrens and sparrows from the nearby willows, all of them in a flutter to have their turn to speak to the gentle mountain. The owls and nighthawks had taken his evening and now it was only fair that they should have his morning to themselves. He must hear of their new nests and warbling chicks and horrid neighbours, and they were going to claim their perches on his head and shoulders and tell him whether he wished to listen or to ignore them accordingly. He would listen, however; the quick and nervous conversation of the sparrows was often one-sided and he was therefore required to do nothing but allow them to nest in his hair and continue walking. The wrens, however, were less content to permit him to be indifferent: they would have him hear of every rude caterpillar and impudent butterfly flitting around trees they knew to be theirs. Theirs was a talk of territory, and they would have Khantara understand their plight. It was wrong of the caterpillars to climb *their* trees and enter *their* nests, and it was so devious of them not to be edible though their bright colours and squirming movements were so enticing. How horrendous it was that the bustle and brilliancy of the butterflies' wings should be so fascinating. They could hardly capture the creatures to feed to their chicks with such a violent display of beauty. Would only Khantara tell the caterpillars to taste more agreeable, the obnoxious moths to make their cocoons somewhere else, and the owls to leave the worms alone when there was mice enough for them. Khantara, however, would say nothing to the purpose. He only smiled and shook his head at the wrens, and their loud and intricate trills conveyed their indefatigable displeasure toward the giant's infuriating civilities. He would let nature go its own way, and the birds could do little to convince him otherwise. The wrens threatened to claim strands of the giant's long molded locks for their nests if he did not comply, but he would not regard their threats as any so troublesome. He simpered at their attempts and silently declared that they could not break his draping tendrils no matter how hard they should try when the giant suddenly found himself at the barracks.

The birds calmed and quieted to hear the chisel of stonecutters and the hammers of carpenters working away. The chief of the work remained in the garrison while most of the training implements had already been completed, but the sounds of the Haanta Amghari availing their apparatuses made the birds tremulous and silent. The whirr of arrows being shot toward Es-Bhostaas targets, the pull and stretch of Rhinghaata ropes, the sway of the wooden Rhakgoskaa beams, the splintering of tree stumps during Khol-Bhisaas, the grunts and shouts of exertion from the Amghari were enough to make the large training area seem rife with activity though many of the Haanta warriors were yet performing their morning meditations. Khantara meant to join them and warned his wrens and sparrows that in a few moments he would be throwing off his shadowcloak and delighting in a match or two before venturing to the barracks. They directly flew back to their trees, fearing the swift motions of Khantara's axe, and left the giant to descend into the training yard.

The warriors sitting in the field finishing their meditations were instantly roused when their gargantuan leader approached; his footfalls were masked by the short dry grass, but his shadow, though lightened by the coming of morning, could not be easily subdued. They stood and bowed in unison and made entreaties for the giant to practice their kaatas with him, and to this, the giant readily agreed. He tossed aside his Dhanna as intended, took his great axe from his back, and called them to match with him one by one. Every warrior fell before his ability, but not without learning of speed or form. They were made to understand that there was a purpose in losing: to improve upon one's talents and become proficient with their given weapons, and Khantara would teach them to be swift in their strikes, elegant in their steps, and strong in their motions even if they must lose to him and to his commanders to learn so vital a lesson.

He passed an agreeable time with the Amghari, training their powers of armed and unarmed combat, when the sun was at last gaining governance over the morning. The last remnants of evening were done away and, much to the chagrin of Amghari, their leader must attend the children at the temple. They shared equal bows to honour their practice together, and when Khantara gathered his cloak from the ground, he observed Jhiaanta coming toward him. The Amhadhri stopped when he reached the Es-Bhostaas targets. His hand lifted to the longbow across his back with unconscious motion, his fingers browsed the fletching of his arrows in their quiver, and he gaped toward the targets in the near distance as if to convey that he could not pass them by without wanting to exercise his prowess with his favoured weapon. His desire, however, was overcome when Khantara overtook him, and he paid his

Odaibha all the attention that was due while making momentary glances to the targets.

Khantara smiled at his keenness. "Practice your bow, Jhiaanta. I will see the progress in the barracks before we leave."

Jhiaanta's eyes were filled with a happy glow but then suddenly dimmed. "The garrison is almost complete, Odaibha, but you will not find Bhaaldhena and Mhardhosa inside." He paused and seemed saddened. "Mhardhosa was unable to restrain himself last night."

"Was Bhaaldhena harmed?" Khantara asked in an earnest tone.

Jhiaanta shook his head. "Mhardhosa was. Bhaaldhena took him to be healed and they went to the temple to assist those who needed help and to wait for you."

Although Mhardhosa's difficulty was well known to everyone, especially to his brothers and Khantara, it did not make the situation any less painful or any less severe than it was. An uncontrollable rage simmered beneath Mhardhosa's reserved exterior, as it did for Haanta men of every distinction, but where others learned to suppress such an affliction, his could not be disciplined. It was violent and incalculable, only quelled by destruction or by the pummelings of his larger brother. Impervious to most harm, Bhaaldhena was the perfect partner for his brother's unbidden rage. This had been established in their youth by Khantara's training them together, and though he has succeeded in helping Mhardhosa to channel his rage in battle, he could not suppress it in its entirety. An evil stain on a gentle and quiet spirit, Mhardhosa could be easier on the peace of the islands than he could be here. There was unrest and detestation that would not be silenced from the Thellisian settlement in the outpost, and Khantara's apprehensions in bringing him to the mainland was in this prevailing disquiet. He could not leave his beloved Amhadhri alone on the islands or exclude him from a war in which his abilities were so greatly needed, but he felt all the wretchedness of the circumstance on Mhardhosa's behalf.

"The mainland disturbs him," Khantara mused. "I feared his affliction would worsen here." He regretted that here his tormented Amhadhri must stay and he was saddened that through all the guidance and attention he had supplied, no ease could be given him from even the mild disturbances of such a strange land. "Come," Khantara said, nodding toward the settlement and resolving to leave his inspection of the barracks for another time now that his Amhadhri's wellbeing was to be looked after. "We will see your brothers at the temple."

To the temple they went, their path enlivened by the Haanta settlement's arousal by sunlight: blacksmiths and leatherworkers were taking to their forges and cutting tables, chandlers and spinners took to their mixing tables and spindles, provisioners went to their stone ovens, and to signify the commencement of the day, the morning hymns were sung. The bards and musicians began their usual procession, their trilling voices and mellifluous harmonies regaling the Haanta people with the words from their scriptures. Their continuous song emanated from the temple and the collective was blanketed by a peaceful hush, everyone saying their quiet daily greetings to one another while listening to the melodies that were to accompany their workday. The song grew more strident when the train of bards and musicians paraded through the slender avenues of the settlement. Everyone was disposed to cease their work and listen to the hymns as they walked by, and even as the bards bowed to Khantara and acknowledged everyone in their path, the only break in their cant was to change from one verse to the next.

With Khantara's awareness deterred by the procession, he had not been prepared for the flurry of children billowing toward the giant when he and Jhiaanta neared the temple entrance. They called out for his attention, pulled the trims of his shadowcloak, and clung to his legs until he would acknowledge them.

"Kodhanaas, Mivaari Leraa," the giant beamed, greeting the eager children collecting around his feet.

"Kodhanaas, Odaibha," their tiny voices sang in unison. They called out for their friends from the temple to join them, and suddenly a deluge of children poured forth from the temple entrance and spilled down the stone steps, all of them racing toward the giant with smiling eyes. They held to his muscular calves, tried to climb his legs, swung from the ends of his hair, and hopped up and down with raised hands begging to be lifted into the giant's arms, all of them asking innumerable questions. "What will you teach us today, Odaibha?" was the prevailing inquiry, first asked by one child and then echoed by the rest.

Khantara was in a glow of fondness for them. He moved aside from the entrance, stepped closer to the garden and sat in the short grass, inviting them to do with him as they would. They climbed into his lap, crawled over his shoulders, hung from his arms and hair and giggled in delight as they tumbled over him. Those who came to the mountain's peak sat atop his shoulders and others fancied themselves content sitting at his sides, but the more they favoured him with their attention, the happier the giant became. They pleaded for him not teach the Amghari in the afternoon that they might have his attention for the entire day, but he simpered and declined their well-meant offers.

"Come, Mivaari," Khantara's voice rumbled, "I will show you something." He collected them all into his lap and lifted his Dhanna over their heads, creating a canopy about their class. "When the Dhanna is held against light, the rays shine through the material." He huddled within the shadowcloak to remark the small shafts of sunlight, hearing the children's attributions of the Dhanna's inside resembling the night sky. They hushed when he began telling them the quiet stories of Ashan, Haanta informants, who chiefly donned such cloaks for their secretive business on the mainland. They listened with perfect attention, cooing in wonder at the operative moments. Some fathomed themselves as Ashan if only to warrant such an article of legend amongst their people, and some protested that they should have one of the cloaks by another means when their small learning encampment was suddenly invaded by the calls of the Themari.

The Haanta priest came racing down the temple steps calling out to the children, "Mivaari, you cannot leave your lessons without saying where you are going." His words were more worried than agitated, but when he observed whose cloak they were hiding under, all the Themari's remonstrances were laid aside. His only fear on their account is that they should venture beyond the borders of their settlement, but as they were in the company of their conqueror and his student, all his apprehensions on the subject diminished. He recollected himself and bowed with civility to his two visitors. "Mivaari, did you honour the Den Amhadhri?" the Themari asked in a warning accent.

The children looked at one another and were ashamed to admit that they had not done as they had learnt to do correctly.

The Themari clapped his hands and the children were suddenly up and forming a line before Khantara. Once they were all in a seemly row, they stood with their hands at their sides and bowed low.

Khantara knew this was a lesson in propriety and respectfulness, but he would treat it as playfully as he could where children were concerned. He felt it right to preserve their innocence and lightheartedness and leave the severities of civility for when they should be older. He tickled their ears and grazed the napes of their necks with the ends of his cloak, forcing them to laugh rather than bow too solemnly. He smiled at the Themari, who though discontent with Khantara's teaching them incorrect manners, deserved a little trouble for the difficulty he created the evening previous. Khantara was about to profess how well the Mivaari bowed when a hawk's cry from above drew his attention. He looked up and greeted his friend circling overhead with a silent and internal welcome. He held his arm out and summoned the creature to him that the children might learn of the creature's majesty and be their morning's lesson.

The hawk obeyed, diving down from the skies with great alacrity, and landed upon Khantara's arm with a flutter of its wings and a clamping of his clawed talons. It preened and stared intermittently, taking a moment to ruffle its brown feathers and another to flick and bob its head as it gazed at the awestruck children. Khantara made a silent entreaty for the creature to allow the children close for a few minutes so that he might enlighten them as to all that was magnificent and humble about the hawk, and the bird agreed for the price of a fish if there was one to be had. The bird was obliged with one of the fish from the pond in the temple garden, and the children were called to gather around it while it ate.

The Mivaari were all attention with wide eyes and opened mouths as Khantara broadened their understanding: how the hawk hunted, how it was said to be the most opportunistic predators in the family of birds, how it ate and how it scavenged was all of immense interest to them. They were permitted to touch its feathers and remark its astonishing wingspan while learning of its flight, gaining more than just the attention of the children as the lesson endured. Soon herb-gatherers and gardeners approached and listened; even the Themari was enthralled, but while everyone belonging to the temple was engaged with Khantara's lesson, Jhiaanta slipped quietly away and went to find his brothers within the temple.

A whisper and a bustle by way of one of the temple attendants brought Mhardhosa and Bhaaldhena to the temple entrance. Both the Amghari had been assisting the carpenters and masons by holding and lifting the immense stone blocks to be used in the temple's inner sanctum, and though they had sustained no injuries in the push and pull of the exertion, Jhiaanta perceived that they had wounds from their duel the evening before: Mhardhosa's forearms were bandaged in various places and Bhaaldhena maintained a few bruises on his face.

"Are you well, brother?" Jhiaanta said softly to Mhardhosa.

"He is now that he has expelled his ethnaa on me," Bhaaldhena interposed.

Jhiaanta regarded Mhardhosa's severe expression and then turned back to Bhaaldhena. "Was slashing his arms necessary?"

"It was to have him drop his weapon."

"I am well, brother," said Mhardhosa grimly. He looked passed Jhiaanta to spy Khantara in the near distance. He calmed, managed to almost smile, but was interrupted by the blithesome sounds of the children around his master calling for more.

"He cannot resist," Bhaaldhena said with a shake of his head.

"No, he cannot, nor should he. We were fortunate to have him as an Odaibha. There are many other Odaibha who are not as patient or as lenient as he is."

Bhaaldhena folded his arms and made a sly look to his brothers. "He would never admit to it, but I think he enjoys the look on the Themari's face when he interrupts lessons."

"Our Odaibha is not vindictive," said Mhardhosa heatedly.

"Perhaps not, but why else would we have been asked to assist in the temple when there are many others who can do the same? Our master wants to be certain that our Mivaari are being taught correctly. You were treated unfairly, Mhardhosa. Have you forgotten?"

Pained by the remembrance, Mhardhosa turned away and made no answer.

Bhaaldhena humphed and narrowed his gaze as he judged the Themari against his master. "He does not need to be here, nor did he need to be at the temple on Mhavhaledhran. He enjoys our Mivaari for many reasons, but he does not trust the Themari to teach them kindness and compassion after he saw how wrongly they had treated you." He glanced at Mhardhosa and his appearance hardened when looking back at the Themari. "His is right to make certain it should never happen again. He worries nearly as much as you do, Jhiaanta, only he does not express it as often."

Jhiaanta gave his brother a flat look. He could not help his cautious nature, and as it had done well for him, he had no contention to make on the subject.

"Come, we will attend him."

And attend him they did.

The moment they descended the temple steps, the Mivaari were called back to their lessons within the auspices of the temple, and where the children bowed to their teacher and followed the Themari back inside, the Amhadhri bowed to their master in welcome and told him of what work was remaining around the temple.

Mhardhosa noticed his master's prying looks toward his injuries and turned his face aside. "I am well, Odaibha," he said in a nervous voice, feeling less well than he professed himself.

Khantara placed his free hand on his student's shoulder and said in a gentle voice, "If you are not, Mhardhosa, you must not be ashamed to tell me."

Mhardhosa only bowed and remained silent.

As the assessment for the morning had been made and the students had been seen, Khantara's mind instantly thought of his visit to Anelta. He could see her for a meal and return in more than enough time to finish his duties in the barracks, but as he considered his visit, his eyes caught a shadow in the doorway of the temple: it was the shade of a small child, one peering toward him from behind the stone archway and endeavoring to take one last peek at the bird on his arm. "Wait here," he said, walking toward the temple.

As the hawk was well-fed and much admired, it was disposed to make one more allowance: Khantara requested that he be allowed to take him into the temple for the young Mivaari who was so desirous of having one last look at it. The bird complied with a nonchalant shrug, and when they came to the stone archway, the hawk was indifferent to the boy's shaking legs and ardent stares.

The child was much smaller than those who had crowded around the giant. He had seen the hawk swoop down while he was on his way to his studies and could not move from the entrance until he had seen the creature closely, or at least until had seen it fly away again. Now, however, in the presence of such a splendid predator, he felt his small courage failing him and could not approach what all the other children had been privileged to see. Where there was both trepidation and childlike zeal for the bird, his apprehension had overcome him, but his curiosity had prevented him from leaving, and he could only gawp in amazement.

"Come, Mivaari," Khantara purred, kneeling to the child. "I know you wish to see. There is no need to fear him. He is honoured to visit us." He beckoned him with an outstretched arm, and within a few moments, the boy was within the bend of the giant's arm and touching the bird's downy chest.

Bhaaldhena half-smiled at his master's perfect approach and scoffed at how effortless his compassion made everything seem.

"Do not mock him," Mhardhosa growled, mistaking his brother's smile.

"I was not mocking him, only admiring his abilities." Bhaaldhena marked his master's care with a gleam in his eye. "If only the Themari had his forbearance."

But if only would not do where the damage had already been done.

DISPARITY

The scent of fresh Sindhaas, the spiced bread eaten by the children and priests at the temple, returned Khantara's thoughts to Anelta. She might be hungry by this time of the day even with a whole Phoraas to recommend her satiation. He could be under no mistake that the stress she incurred from her loneliness and rejection was as taxing to her body as it was to her mind, and where one Phoraas might do for a warrior, one who had been trained into an excellent constitution, it might not do for one of her condition.

Now that his duties for the morning had done, Khantara said his goodbyes and his thanks to the hawk, entreated it to fly where it would, and went with his Amhadhri to the provisioner for more food to bring to Anelta. He requested grains and breads, vegetables and herbs, everything that was needed to sustain her before her mate should return. The provisioner, though near the temple, was also near the Thellisian markets, still within the Haanta settlement but close enough that a mere copse of trees was all that divided the two nations from one another here, and while the package was being prepared for Khantara's conveyance, he and the three Amhadhri were suddenly drawn by sounds coming from the section of the markets where the Thellisian stalls were situated.

A young boy, no older than five years of age, was attempting to break free from his father's hold. The marketplace was alive with its usual crowds, and the boy was being secured by the hand while his eyes went everywhere and his finger pointed at everything. His curiosity was tolerated until the father required both hands free to carry a parcel away from one of the stalls, and the instant the boy's hand was let go, he hurried over to everyone and everything he could. He was called, commanded to obey and return to his father, but the boy would go his own way. He must touch everything and say hello to everyone and run about as he chose, but soon the forbearance for his conduct had all but done: when the father took hold of his son again it was only to scold him. The child, being of such an innocent age, had little idea why his father was shouting or why he should not go to the line of trees at the end of the markets, and therefore when he was freed again, he ran immediately to where Khantara and the three Amhadhri were standing.

Khantara knelt and was prepared to welcome the giggling boy into his arms when the child was suddenly pulled back by the arm and struck by his father. Laughter turned into cries, smiles became tears, and as the father demanded his son's compliance, he dragged him off to his mother whilst trying to impress the danger in which the child had placed himself. Such indelicacy, such ill-conduct toward one who would learn from an elder's example was an atrocity that Khantara could not abide. To harm in defense of oneself was one thing, but to reprimand in such a manner, and where it was hardly necessary, was entirely another; the fear that the father may have had toward himself was understandable, but the reaction could not be excused, for the child had done nothing but mind his curiosity and now he would learn that exploring was wrong.

Khantara stood from his place and said in a grave drone, "I pity the Dhargovhari." He paused, looked toward the father and the child in the distance, and presently added, "I pity their Mivaari more."

He sighed that it must be so, that their nations must perhaps be forever divided, but the poignant lesson he had learned was a pang to his sensibilities. The disparity of treatment between his nation and theirs, the former treating children with kindness and leniency and the latter disciplining and dominating, was a saddening prospect. Would Thellis have treated their own well, he should be easy with leaving them to govern one another as they liked, but this confirmed all his reservations with regard to Thellis. They refused to join with the Haanta in peace, and worse: they treated one another with such animosity. Even those who were too young to understand their transgressions seemed to be given punishments that only the most violent of Haanta malefactors would incur. Teaching the child the reason their nations did not interact would have been more constructive, but the father's agitation hindered him from being edifying and now the child must suffer.

Khantara shook his head and seemed out of charity with himself. He wished he would have said something, but he feared an interruption would have caused more harm to the child than good. He made a heavy sigh and said to his Amhadhri, "They believe that *we* are the crueler nation, yet they would attack their own Mivaari and enslave their own women."

Bhaaldhena and Jhiaanta looked at one another and then turned back to their master, sharing in his disenchantment. Mhardhosa seemed more disquieted than usual. He shifted in place beside his brothers and looked to Khantara with the hopes of comforting him, but there was no consoling the giant.

Between the Marked woman and the crying child, Khantara had seen enough to understand Thellis' prejudice: everyone who did not adhere to the word of a superior was instantly cast down in a horrible light, leaving him to fear for the child's future and to worry for Anelta's. With all the urgency that seeing such a circumstance presented, Khantara took the ready package of breads and grains from the provisioner, excused himself from his Amhadhri, asking them to continue their duties in the barracks, and shuffled toward the lane that led to Anelta's home, that he might do some good for the downtrodden of Thellis if they would not do so for one another.

The Marketplace

ven with his quickened pace, moved by the overpowering desire to aid the Marked woman, Khantara had just missed her. When he came to the small and disheveled house at the end of the lane, he descried Anelta leaving and hastening toward the marketplace with what appeared to be three dresses of decent quality in her hands. He could overtake her from his position behind the trees, but something hindered him and asked him to follow her instead. He requested that the birds adorning his hair and all the small creatures scurrying about his feet remain silent while he slipped into the shadows. By tying the small parcel in his hands to the belt of his worn kilt and wrapping the folds of his Dhanna about him, the immense giant became invisible in the shade.

In the shadows he would remain, using the shade of trees and buildings to screen him from view, masking his footfalls with sideways steps, but he soon found the need for another hiding place when he observed Anelta taking another route to the markets. She seemed to be walking toward the Church, and though he had little idea why she would venture to such a place when she had professed of their cruelty to her kind the day before, he allowed the situation to continue if only to have his curiosity satisfied. He took shelter in some nearby hedges surrounding the Church grounds and watched as Anelta made her approach. A sign hung at the side door of the building, calling all those in need of food and shelter to enter, but as Anelta could not read, she went to the front entrance instead and was about to knock when the side door suddenly opened.

"What are you doing over there, child?" said an old woman, emerging from within the Church. "Come here. You know you aren't allowed to use that entrance."

The old woman's voice did not have the caring tone that one at her time of life should have possessed. She was coarse and irritated, haggard in feature and scornful in temper. Khantara began to worry that Anelta would find no kindness here, and he moved to rescue her when the old woman suddenly began speaking in an elevated voice.

"Again?" she scoffed once Anelta was close. "This is the fourth time this month, child."

"Yes, Reverend Mother," said Anelta dutifully, bowing her head and keeping her eyes low.

The Reverend Mother turned up her hooked nose and waved Anelta on with a flick of her boney hand. "Away with you, child. Sister Leilia has shown you kindness enough in letting you sit at her table and allowing you to share her meal. I saw the apron she gave you last week."

"Yes, Reverend Mother. It was very generous of her to help me—"

"There's nothing here for you today, child," she coldly interposed. "There are others here whose needs are more important than yours."

Anelta, though disheartened, was not disappointed. She had been shown more kindness and forbearance than allowable by the Sisters upon many occasions, but this treatment towards herself was not to be unexpected from their matron. She made no protestation, only bowed her head and clung to the dresses in her hands.

"I don't need to remind you that you have a husband and a home, child. You should be grateful for what he gives you."

"Yes, Reverend Mother. I am."

"He does a great kindness by you, taking you in and providing for you as he does. You ought to thank him for his charity instead of coming here and taking from others. When you ask for what others need, you are stealing from them," the old woman repeated in a slow and condescending tone, speaking to Anelta as though someone of her situation could not understand such a lesson. "Remember that there are always others who are more wretched and disadvantaged than yourself. There are many without shelter and food. Your husband gives you both when I'm certain there are others more worthy of his attention."

"Yes, Reverend Mother," was Anelta's mortified reply.

"And you would do well to remind him of our numerous contributions to you. He too needs a lesson in gratitude if he cannot give goodwill where it is needed."

Anelta turned away. "Yes, Reverend Mother," she said quietly, "I will tell him."

"Are those for donation, child?"

"Pardon, Reverend Mother?"

"Those," said the old woman heatedly, stabbing her finger toward the dresses in Anelta's arms. "Are you at last donating something to the Church after all the kindness we've shown you?"

She must give a decided and negative reply, though she dreaded saying anything other than a polite mentioning of the old woman's title. To say no might bring such a remonstrance that could have her prohibited from returning to the Church when she may need their services most, but to say yes might ruin all her designs of eating for the remainder of the day. She disliked having to apply to such a disagreeable woman for help, but she disliked even more the slender remorse she had been made to feel for those less fortunate than herself. She did have shelter at least; this could not be denied, but she must confess that she would rather have a means of daily sustenance than a roof over her head when there was sky and stars enough in Thellis to act as a suitable sanctuary. She regarded the dresses in her hands, judged which one was the best of the three, and held it out for the Reverend Mother to take, hoping that a donation by any means would warrant a relenting on the Reverend Mother's side. She was wrong, however, for the moment she held out the dress, it was snatched up without a word of thanks, the door to the Church was closed, the old woman was gone, and Anelta was left with fresh compunction to feel, rueful that she had little to give in return for their forbearance.

Acknowledging that she might not be obliged again for some time, Anelta was determined to forget this small measure of unkindness and continue toward the marketplace where her remaining two dresses could be traded for some oats, which could be saved and stored for whenever she was in need of something to eat when her husband should be detained in town. She had kept some in the pantry until a few days prior when he had suddenly come home and demanded a supper while she had been left with little means to supply one. A scolding and a few caustic words were her punishment for being so paltry a provider, but where she had appeased him, she had brought vexation to herself. Seldom could she save a copper or two aside for an urgent situation, and an empty pantry and lean larder were ever distressing sights. One copper could yield little more than a leek, two would merit some onions and garlic, but five would fetch grain and the smallest catch from the fishmonger, and in selling what few possessions she had, her aspirations resided in bargaining for five copper at least.

To the Thellisian side of the markets Anelta went. She had little idea of her being followed, and even less of her being followed by Khantara, but even if the giant had stepped from his place in the shadows to address her, she would not have noticed. The marketplace was all her delight: the blurring movement of the crowds, the vibrant hues of the tents and stalls, the strident calls of the sellers, the variety of items, the blend of Livanon and Thellisian faces, the few sprinklings of Lucentians, the openness of the square; everything ordered her to stop and remark the whirr of sound and motion about her, and though she saw other Marked men and women being ignored by buyers or shooed away by traders, she must smile and feel that however mistreated she may have been, she could not feel dejected in such a place as this. So much went on and there were so many people about her as to make her completely forget any injustice towards herself. Here was a magical place, one where everything might be got for a price, where conversation was open, where remonstrances had purpose, and where there was no Reverend Mother or husband or master to ridicule her. Here she was free to gawp and stroll as she would with only the rumblings of her stomach to hurry her steps. She could bear starvation if this was to be her reward: a place to go, people to see, flowers to smell, fabric to remark; the house was so unprepossessing where the marketplace had every means of attraction.

Khantara saw her enchantment in her slow strides and smiling aspect. Her cheeks were in a glow of animation, her eyes sparkling with joy, she seemed nearly to skip as she went toward the Thellisian stalls. He observed her walk toward the textile merchants, saying hello to those who cared to look at her and begging the pardon of those who were blocking her way toward one of the textile traders. Khantara hoped that this meeting would produce a more favourable result than the one he had witnessed at the Church. He inched closer and wondered why she did not go to the Haanta traders at the other end of the marketplace. There she would be treated with equality and kindness, and though he felt that not every Thellisian must see the Marked in the same light, he would be more at ease if she sought his people for attention.

She was getting too close to the trader now to follow her with tolerable secrecy. The buzzing of the markets was too great to hear Anelta's gentle voice, and if he wished to continue his vigil, he would have to make use of an agent to assist his efforts. Khantara narrowed his gaze and looked about the marketplace grounds. In the centre of the square, he saw a small birdbath with a collection of wrens round it, drinking from the cultivated rainwater and preening their feathers. He beckoned to them with his mind. Their heads turned, they chirruped in answer, but only one of them came to him without further provocation. It was a fey wren, a small and exquisite bird with bright blue feathers, black beak, long stiff tail and pleasant chirp. It fluttered toward Khantara's raised finger and perched upon him, ruffling his downy plumes and sidling up to him to show his allegiance.

"I have a special task for you, Bhontaa," Khantara purred, stroking the feathers of the bird's neck. "There is someone I need you to follow and I need you to repeat to me everything that is said between her and those to whom she speaks. Are you able to do that?"

The bird cooed and chirped that it would be more than happy to fulfill such an office in exchange for serving so noble a master.

"If you do well, I will reward you by making you my companion. The woman there," he said, pointing to Anelta, "needs our assistance, and we must do everything we can to make certain that she is cared for. Do you agree to help me?"

The bird hopped and twittered.

"*Haa*," said Khantara with a smile. "There is a tree beside the merchant. Sit on the lowest bough and tell me what is said. If she is sent away from the stall, you must follow her."

The wren went directly to the branch Khantara marked. It sat and pretended to preen itself when it heard the conversation between the woman and the trader suddenly commence.

Anelta was welcomed to the trader's booth with a forthcoming smile. She stepped forward when she was bid to approach, bowed and waited to be addressed.

"Well," said the trader, "what may I do for you, *koebita*?" said the trader.

Anelta's complexion warmed to be called anything so pleasant in Thellisian. Though he had only accorded her a common designation for a young and supposedly unmarried woman, it had been a liberty never before taken with her. "I was wondering, sir, if you might appraise these for me."

"Are you here to trade or sell, *koebita*?"

"Sell, sir."

"Then, let us have a look."

He bid her to lay the items on the table before him. He began his examination, scrutinizing the thinness of the cloth to see how much of its quality had been worn away from wear. He passed his fingers over the grain, placed his hand between the layers, held the folds of the material up to the sun, judged the vibrancy of the hues and value of the dyes employed, inspected the lining for any tears and nicks, and in conclusion of his investigation, he said, "I'm sorry, *koebita*, but these are not in excellent condition."

"I know, sir," said Anelta softly, "but they are all I have besides the one I am wearing."

The trader observed her dress and saw that it was in an even worse state than the two she had laid upon his table. He sighed and felt for her, and after some postulation said, "I suppose I can have these cut into swatches. I can give you four copper for them, two for each, but any more than that and I'm losing money."

Four was not five, but it was certainly better than one or nothing at all. She knew he was being generous with her, and if only she had not given her third and most valuable dress to the Reverend Mother, she might have been able to fetch six copper or even more. She must be satisfied with five; it was more than enough to secure her one day's meal if not two, and if she could buy some grain and a small bit of honey, she might have porridge enough for a few days hence. She was almost inclined to accept the man's offer, but something within her urged her to bargain with him. "Might it be five, sir?"

The trader was about to respond with a firm shake of the head, but her dry lips, pallid skin, thin frame, and hungry eyes hindered him from giving an immediate answer. There was no pretending here; her deprivation and undernourishment was obvious, and though he was not the wealthiest of traders, what was one more copper to him when the difference to someone else meant eating for two days instead of one? He would make up for such a paltry loss by the end of the day, and therefore five was to be his price. He was agreeing and taking the five coppers from his pocket when he suddenly stopped to remark the brand on the woman's neck. His smiles faded, his countenance altered, and all the friendliness with which he had hitherto treated her was over. "Why did you come to my stall, *znaconei?*" he sibilated, his features growing stern and angry.

She knew it was too fortunate to find a trader who would accept her presence so unquestionably. She had thought to tell him before laying the dress down for his appraisal, but she was too pleased to be received to regard her apprehensions. Now she would pay for the omission with her embarrassment, and she could only hope he would not speak quite so loud or use such a hateful designation again. "I came to give you business, sir," she said in a half-whisper.

"I do not serve your kind, *znaconei*, nor do any of the traders in this row. Take your items and leave before I report you to the guards."

"But, I'm married, sir. I'm permitted to go to the markets on my own."

"You may be," said the trader carelessly, "but that doesn't mean I will willingly accept your scraps. If you want charity, go to the Church. Take your things and leave my stall before anyone thinks I'm trading

with you."

Anelta felt betrayed by his previous benevolence but blamed herself for expecting too much from someone whom she had only just met. The giant, who had so lately filled her thoughts, had ruined her for conversation: though *he* had spoken to her with openheartedness and entreated her to do the same, she must remember her place and must remember that no one else had been used to speak to her with such consideration before his arrival. "Thank you for your conversation, sir," she said to the trader in a mechanical murmur. "It was kind of you to speak to me. I'm sorry for disturbing you." She took her garments from the table, bowed low, and hurried away, looking up to the skies to stifle the tears she felt bursting on her.

Appalled and disillusioned by such needless cruelty, Khantara decided that he would no longer skulk about in the shadows. He would show himself if only to command some measure of respect for the desperate woman. He nodded to the wren, ordering him to fly after Anelta, and as the bird hopped from tree to tree in chase of her, Khantara emerged from his place in the shade and walked toward the stalls to impress his stature and prowess upon merchants and crowds. Such terrorizing tactics were not his way, but he had seen the disregard of which these merchants were unfortunately capable and he must retaliate where he could: he would frighten them into sympathy if he must, and the instant he emerged from behind the outer wall of the open market, there was an end to all peace in the place. Merchants awed at the sight of him, patrons fled in terror, parents stared and clung to their children, women gasped and flocked away, and though he did not enjoy striking fear into the Thellisian masses, he took particular consolation in glaring at the trader who had rejected Anelta and almost smiled to see him cowering beneath his table and whimpering for mercy.

The giant's appearance raised a great deal of alarm, so much so that the guards standing and observing the goings-on placed their hands on their weapons and were prepared to defend their people if necessary, but as the shuffling mountain did little else other than tread at a slow pace in quest of a Marked woman, they thought it advisable to remain at their stations and not expatiate the general anxiety. They only watched with reserved looks as the giant pursued the woman to the square. He seemed ill-disposed to catch her, however; she stopped at the small fountain in the square to wash her crimsoned face and red eyes, and he remained a few paces behind as though waiting for her to continue forward toward the Lucentian or Haanta sections of the market.

When cupping her hands and gathering the fresh water into her palms, Anelta stopped a moment to regard herself in the reflection in the pool's surface. Was she so very horrible and disgusting? Must she be so disagreeable to everyone? She felt an inundation of confusion: if her presence was so troublesome to most, why had the giant been so eager to speak with her? Surely one of his consequence—for he must be significant in the Haanta society with such a peaceful air and lofty stature—should be repelled by one so objectionable as herself. Why had he shown her civilities and generosity that was wanting everywhere else was a question which plagued her as she washed her face and dried her eyes with the hem of her dress. She breathed deeply, listening to the tinkling din of the fountain and the trilling chirps of the birds. She closed her eyes and felt the coolness in her cheeks revive her composure. She attempted to do away with any notions of unworthiness; there must be something about her that was worthy of regard, for why else would the giant have sat with her and shared his meal with her and permitted her to touch him without reproach— she checked herself before her tears could resurface. These were pleasurable and painful musings only interrupted by the fervent chirrups of a blue fey wren sitting on the edge of the fountain. Her frown curled into a soft smile, her head tilted slightly, and she marveled as the creature sang and hopped about. It must be a trick of the mind, but to her, it seemed as though it was trying on purpose to gain her attention. It danced and fluffed its feathers, and it inched its way off the fountain toward the canopied stalls of the Haanta trading pavilion.

She followed the bird as it flew to the arched entranceway. "And why should I not enter," was her first consideration as she peered past the threshold. "He was so kind to me. Maybe the others will be kind as well?" She said it more to convince herself of walking into the small pavilion, screened from the sun by brilliant and colourful draping silks and filled with the quietness of the Haanta traders speaking their low words to one another. A few of them made momentary glances at her, thinking that she would near and that they would have someone to serve, but she only waited at the entrance, agonizing over whether there were specific regulations not only for the Marked but also for Thellisians to enter without a Haanta attendant. She knew little of the history between their nations; she only knew that this section of the empire was now occupied and that those Thellisians who were free to learn and live as they would disliked having the race of quiet giants even beside them. Rumbles of a hungry stomach compelled her to enter at last, and if she was to be ejected from the Haanta trade pavilion, then she will have been removed having seen the mysteries prevalent within its silken walls.

A trove of wonders was presented her as she passed the beginning threshold. The fey wren had flown in after her and flitted about, guiding her gaze from table to table. She was stopped by the friendly smiles afforded her from the various Haanta traders. She was astonished to discover that they were all different from one another: each Haanta of varying and soaring heights, each with a dissimilar skin and eye colours, each with intricate hairstyles and simple linen clothes. Their wares, too, were diverse and miraculous to her: gold and silver laid out in pyramidal bars, ores and precious stones displayed on black velvet along the ground, shells and glass trinkets reflecting the sunlight as they hung from the high beams, fabrics of every hue and make, flowers and fruit-- everything to recommend the wealth of the islands was exhibited before her, and even more curious was the Haanta's eagerness to have her examine anything she was desirous of seeing. There was remarkable serenity here, suggested by the uncommon silence and the rays of sunlight invading the cracks in the pavilion canopy. Upon perceiving all this, she wondered at why there were not more Thellisians inspecting the aisles when there was such tranquility to be suffered and such beauty to be seen.

She was yet unaware, but Anelta herself was an article of immense interest. To the Haanta traders who scarcely saw any Thellisian enter the pavilion—especially a woman and one alone—she was a welcome prospect. They had been used to serve only those who were in want of their gold and silver, though they had brought many other items of value for trade, and had been used to only serve Lucentians, for the elven neighbours of Thellis had been friends of the Haanta these fifty years and were no stranger to their part of the markets or to the trade port of the islands. A Thellisian woman, however, one as tall, as striking, as threadbare and as nervous as Anelta was a most fascinating view. Even more so was Khantara, who had entered the canopied area after the woman and had garnered much in the way of low bows and murmured greetings when he passed the stalls. The traders' solicitations were silenced with a small gesture from their supreme commander, indicating that he was following Anelta without her knowledge. They nodded and busied themselves about their booths while spying the woman's timorous movements as she weaved in and out of the rows, according every table its due consideration with happy agitation.

Anelta made polite bows and smiles to everyone who granted her the same. Here there were many who were attentive and obliging, all waiting to tend to her with keen eyes and hands outstretched. There was much about the traders to mesmerize her, but the lack of Haanta women was the object most concerning. She wondered where they were if not here, and she wondered if they were permitted to leave the protection of the Haanta settlement just as she had been forbidden to wander beyond the borders of the Church and the markets. She deemed all of the men shorter than Khantara yet they were still much taller than herself. Their willingness to assist and serve her soon made her easy, and when she felt equal to addressing one of the broad-shouldered, tremendous traders, one with blue-grey skin, black hair, and violet eyes with stacks of various materials and textiles laid out on the table before him, she approached and held up her dresses for evaluation.

"Kodhanaas, sister," said the trader with a cordial bow.

Anelta gave a small start. She was struck with such familiarity, and from someone of another race to give her such a title was pleasing as it was unpredicted. "Sister," she repeated. "But, I'm Thellisian, sir."

The trader smiled at her simple misunderstanding and entreated her to come closer to the table. "How may I assist you?"

She was about to place the dresses down upon the table when her eye caught a braid of horsehair hanging from the end of the stall. It was tied with a silver band and decorated with what she assumed must be Haanta inscriptions. It did not look unlike her own hair, and where she might have received a few copper for her dresses, a braid as long and as exquisite as hers, though thick and somewhat coarse, might be as valuable to the Haanta as it was to Thellis. She placed the dresses aside and took the end of her long braid in hand. She considered what it would be like to lose the one item she had forever kept with her, but where a hungry stomach was concerned, she could do very well without hair half so long. "Excuse me, sir," she began, holding her hair up for display. "I was wondering, how much would you be able to give me for this?"

The trader grimaced and stared at Anelta with surprise. "You would wish to sell that? I cannot take it from you, sister. It is too valuable."

Anelta's eyes brightened. She had mistook his meaning when he said that something so commonplace should be so prized, and holding her hair toward him, she pleaded, "Please, sir. Please tell me how much it's worth."

Such a precious item could have no marketable price, but just before the trader could give an informative reply, a shadow cast over Anelta and obliged her to turn round. She looked up and saw the blue wren flitting toward Khantara's shoulder. She beamed to see the giant coming toward her, and before she could even speak his name, he was bowing to her, he was taking her hand and pressing it with earnest conviction.

"We do not sell our pride, Anelta," Khantara thrummed. "Our Khopra, our bodies, are sacred. We honour them for carrying our Salhiika, our souls, and therefore we should treat them with respect."

He was holding her hand: here was a notion to delight and discomfit her. She was aware of his speaking to her, but his warmth, the pleasing roughness of his hands, the manner in which her fingers curled about his thumb bemused and silenced her. She could say nothing beyond a breathless "Yes, sir," to acknowledge his instruction, and do little else other than gape at him with a rapidly warming complexion.

Khantara's forwardness was purposeful, but he was sensible of its being requisite for her to comprehend the seriousness of the offense she had almost committed. A mane so exquisite and distinguishing as hers might fetch a high price with a Thellisian or a Lucentian merchant, but here under the auspices of the Haanta banner, her hair was too sacred and therefore her pride was impregnable. He would not allow her to beg for what should be her right from birth, the rights of sustenance and care, and after a moment of partial smiles and rubbing the back of her hand with his thumb, he turned to the trader and said, "Ghaandhari, you are not to take anything this woman offers you. Treat her as one of us and be generous with her if she asks for assistance."

"Of course, Vhessel Dhoss-hi," said the trader, graciously inclining his head.

Anelta was shaken from her state upon hearing the odd designation Khantara was supplied. He had not told of this one, and she began to wonder at its meaning. She wondered at if it were the more correct title she should be using, and became nervous when she realized that every Haanta in the immediate area was bowing in agreement to Khantara's order. He *was* of great consequence, perhaps even more than she had hitherto conceived, to be giving such a charge and to obey without question. Her fretfulness was soon done away when the giant leaned down to her and said in a soothing hum:

"Come," and ushering her forward added, "Show me what you need and I will make certain you have it."

This was too much charity to endure. He had nothing to gain by treating her with such unmitigated and unbidden generosity, and she was diffident to assent to his offer. So decidedly lower than himself, and yet he was touching her arm and supplicating to her as though they were equals. She felt a pang of culpableness rush on her; she could not take what was not hers, and here she would be queried many times over to point and ask for things that should never be hers. She would govern herself, though the tears in her eyes betrayed her overpowering sentiments, and she would only choose what was needed to sustain her until her husband should return to their house and all this agreeable reverie should be over. She walked through the rows of the pavilion as the giant insisted and screened her tears from him with her hand though she could not mask the soft sounds of her sobs.

Trading

any of the Haanta traders endeavored to look away as the weeping woman passed their stalls to spare her the humiliation her tears may have garnered. They wondered if she were somehow afraid of the immense conqueror at her back, but when they saw the torn hem of her dress and her bare feet, they were all too aware of the reason for her tears. She was yet another victim of Thellis, and they were only too pleased and relieved to see their supreme commander take her by the hand and lead her toward where the provisioners were stationed.

Every effort was made to calm the Marked woman: the fey wren flew down from his master's shoulder and sang and hopped about for her; everyone in the pavilion, even the Lucentian tradesmen who had come in quest of incense and precious stones gave way to her and smiled, but at last it was the serenity in Khantara's vivid yellow and black eyes that forced her to recompose. She was stricken with a moment's hesitation when she observed the abundance of food near the granary and small mill at the end of the row, but though in her apprehension she stopped and thought to absent herself, she was impeded by the giant's immense form and his entreaty stay.

"Stay among my people," he said softly, guiding her steps ahead. "You may not know them, but they will treat you with fairness."

Anelta looked about her and saw that silver trinkets, shelled necklaces and sandalwood combs were being held out to her from every direction. "But they are offering me things without payment. I cannot take what is not mine," she begged, her chest swelling with the onset of fresh tears.

Khantara pressed her hand to calm her as he guided her through the multitude of lavish displays adorning the Haanta tables. "You are not taking. We are giving."

Anelta hardly knew where to begin on the regulations impressed upon the Marked with regard to gifts. She was forbidden to receive them from anyone other than the one to whom she belonged, and if *he* would not make her a present of suitable dress or even tolerable shoes, how was she to accept the indulgence of others? She agonized in silence and began turning back, hoping to walk unnoticed toward the entrance again, but Khantara would have her continue and his wren would command her to stay under his master's watch.

Though the wren was of superior understanding and did not waste time discussing what worms he found or how quickly he could build a nest in a tree, he was determined to be heard on other points. The moment he felt Anelta's uneasiness increase, he floated down before her eyes and cried and canted until she was diverted enough to forget about absenting. He was unaware that Anelta could not make sense of his coos and crows; his master understood him well enough, and therefore he surmised that everyone must hear and comprehend him. He made every justification in the world for her never to return to the Thellisian side of the markets again though his chirps were answered with looks of vast bewilderment on Anelta's side.

Khantara simpered and allowed the bird to make his warbling pleas until his chirps became moderate again. "This is my sentinel," said he, smiling. He presented his new companion by having the wren perch upon his finger. "We were watching you for some time, Anelta," he quietly confessed.

Anelta coloured deeply and held her hand to her cheek. "Oh," she exhaled, sinking in mortification. "I hope you didn't . . . that is—I didn't know you were . . ." She stopped for breath and lowered her eyes. "Had I known, I would not have—But, how is it possible that I didn't notice? How did you—?"

"I was well-hidden." His gentle interposition was not what had silenced her; the hand that he held against his chest was what had quieted all notions of embarrassment and gave way to very different feelings exposed by the rising colour in her cheeks. "I am well-trained in the art of Dhovhola and have learned to hide myself even in light. However, it was difficult for me to remain hidden once we reached the marketplace. I needed his assistance, and as you see, he is more than pleased to be with us."

He bid the wren to go to Anelta, and the eager creature did his part so well as to make her smile by landing at the top of her braid and sliding down its length. He then crept up her braid, alternating the clench of his beak and grip of his small talons, until he reached her shoulder.

She curled into the nape of her neck as the tips of the bird's wings dusted her cheeks and laughed as he began nestling against her. "He's so beautiful," she said, marveling at the deep hue of his blue feathers.

"He thanks you," said Khantara, browsing the top of the wren's head with his fingertips. "He says that if you had not moved away from the Thellisian trader when you did, he would have done something unpleasant to defend your honour."

Anelta was obliged to laugh until she suddenly stopped and realized, "You are able to understand what birds say?" She gave a start, but it was a start of wonderment and delight, not one of misgiving. Her eyes brightened, and she beamed at him as though asking for proof of such a miraculous claim.

He appeased her curiosity with a quiet beckoning to the birds around and near the pavilion. Suddenly, through the entrance and through the cracks in the silk canopy came a flurry of birds, all of them diving toward Khantara's open hand with a blur of colour. They tweeted and strutted about, displaying themselves one by one with open wings and haughty airs, the most colourful and the longest feathered striving to exhibit first along the length of Khantara's arm, and those of less outward beauty content to perform their trills whilst awaiting their turn.

Anelta owned herself enchanted, did not know when she had ever been so delighted, clapped her hands together to give due acclamation and thanks to the birds for attending Khantara's call. She was all wonder and felicity, and had therefore forgotten every idea of leaving the pavilion.

"They accompany me when I am away from my people in the late evenings," said the giant, giving a slow nictation to his object. "They enjoy telling me of how they make their nests among other things."

"It must be wonderful to have such companions all the time," was Anelta's breathless exclamation as she spied every one of the glorious creatures adorning the giant's shoulders.

Some sentiments of loneliness must here be felt for Anelta, for Khantara saw the momentary dimming in her countenance when she said it. She must long to speak to anyone during days so long and forlorn with nothing to do but be imprisoned in a disagreeable home with no one to speak to beyond what fleeting idle discussion the few Marked in the marketplace could afford. He wished that she could be transferred the gift that was his from birth if only to provide her with a wealth of supernumerary discourse to furnish every moment. He sighed that it could not be so, and the only thing to do for her was to care for her as no one else hitherto had done.

"Come," he purred, ushering Anelta to the end of the row. "Walk before me and I will follow you. Do not be afraid to ask my people for what you may need. They know that you are my guest here."

"But I must give them something in return for their items," said Anelta, looking down at the dresses in her hands.

"Keep them, Anelta. My people have no need for currency of any kind."

Anelta would not have refuted him after seeing such wealth exhibited so openly except that in passing one of the rows, she observed a tall and sleek-looking Lucentian merchant exchanging royal Lucentian notes for a few bars of gold. "Then, why do your people trade if not for money?"

"To obtain information and to learn of the people around us," Khantara explained, nodding to one of the provisioners before him and pointing to a few sacks of milled grain. "Most of my people do not leave our settlement. We therefore must use our time in the markets to discover what we can of the other nations here on the mainland." He took the few sacks of grain, thanked and bowed to the provisioner and helped Anelta along to the next table to retrieve some of the fruits and vegetables cultivated from the settlement. "What you see there," he said, leaning down and motioning significantly to the Lucentian walking from table to table and exchanging notes without receiving much in return, "is an agent sent to us by Prince Lamir of Lucentia. He is giving a few of the Ghondaari, or traders, information about Thellis that we will take to our Hakriyaa, the leader of our armies."

"Your traders are allowed to address your leader?" said Anelta in a whirl of confusion as she watched the giant take a week's worth of produce from the provisioner.

"They are, but some of the traders you see are not traders at all."

"Then, what are they, may I ask?"

Khantara lowered his voice, and placing his procured items in the bend of his arm said, "They are scouts. They observe and report everything they see to the Hakriyaa."

"Thellis is being watched?" said Anelta in a half-whisper, uncertain if she were pleased or horrified by the realization.

"It is," he replied, nodding toward the flat breads at the end of the nearest table and gaining a few for his hand. Receiving most of what he felt Anelta should require, he was eager to hurry her along toward the opposing end of the pavilion where the various leathers from the islands were being displayed. "There is no need for concern," he said, passing a few of the items in his hands to Anelta. "We do not mean to conquer your capital, but your emperor believes we do, which is why information must be exchanged in secret."

Anelta supposed she understood though she knew little of these matters. War, business, and even dislike for the Haanta were a mystery to her. Even more mysterious was how the Haanta survived as an independent nation when they seemed to give away everything that was precious according to mainland profession.

"Our people have everything we need," he assured her. "Everyone on the islands is given food and shelter, and everyone performs his and her Mivaala, or purpose, to improve and support the lives of others. The notes you see being exchanged go to our scouts. Though this form of currency is not needed on the islands or in the settlement, it is needed to sustain them while they live away from the care of my people."

He ceased his explication when he was suddenly forced to stand aside and make way for a consignment of gold being conveyed through the row they were currently in. He stepped back and took Anelta with him, but she was ill-prepared for being taken aside and tripped over the giant's large feet. She fell against him, gripped his torn kilt to maintain her balance, but in doing so had placed her hand in between his legs, and though the touch was slight and admittedly not unpleasant, she was mortified for not having grabbed somewhere higher for leverage. She made her profuse apologies when she righted, but in looking up was given the most affable and warmhearted of smiles. She suddenly became aware of being pressed against him as the conveyers passed; her chest against his abdomen, her thighs against his shins. She felt a warm blush wave over her. She must look away from him, but she was craning her neck, he was leaning down to her, and before she could possibly discomfit herself further, the conveyers had passed, she stood back, and only the imprint of the giant's warmth was left upon her. She could hardly breathe under such pleasurable distress. She could only look down and command her trembling hands to be still.

Soon she had more humiliation to feel, for in her state of happy confusion and discomfited pleasance, she had not been prepared for the giant's kneeling down and lifting one of her bare feet. She gasped in horror to see him placing the sole of what seemed to be a sandal under her heel, and before she could react, he was placing her foot down, holding it there with his toes, and lacing the long leather straps around her ankle and calf. "Oh, no, please," she said in a tremulous voice, nearly dropping the items in her hand upon the ground. "I cannot accept them."

"We do not refuse gifts," said Khantara firmly, lifting her other leg and performing the same motions. "To do so is to greatly shame the giver." He stood and spied the sandals, remarking how well they looked and how prettily they framed her tall and slender legs.

To feel something upon her feet was an endless joy to Anelta. Her mumblings of how she could not possibly accept so handsome a gift began to quiet the longer she wore them. Perhaps she could accept them where traveling to the Church and market was concerned, but if *he* should see them and inquisition her as to where she got them, what truth could she say that he might believe? It was nonsense to reason with one who was constantly reminding her of the regulations in place to keep her where she was, and though she may have wished with all her soul to keep them, even if only to do so as a reminder of the kindness she had been once paid, she could not without immense vexation. "Please," she whispered with a quivering lip, "I can't accept them." She paused and recollected. "He will ask who has given them to me. If I lie to him and tell him that I found them in the poor basket at the Church, he will know."

Khantara already disliked this *he*. Every one of Anelta's meager comforts was dependent upon *he*, and though the giant knew not his name or his true nature, *he* mistreated and ill-used this unexceptionable creature, and that was reason enough to dislike him. He saw the conflict Anelta felt in her ever-changing features, at one moment daring to be happy and gratified for her gift and at another sinking into the terrors of her impending punishment. "I will return to your home with you," he decided, "and I will wait with you until he returns." The giant contrived to explain the finer points on gift-giving to Anelta's husband with addition of instructing him in the proper methods of how to treat a mate with honour.

Anelta knew not whether to thank or to refute the giant's assertion. She wished him to return to her home that she might make him a meal to express her appreciation the only manner in which she knew how, but as they left the pavilion and walked away from the markets, with sandals on her feet and several items in hand, fresh agitation overpowered her and she sincerely hoped that the two men would never meet for fear of the giant's reaction if they should.

An Extended Visit

His duties at the barracks must be deferred, and though it cost Khantara some feelings of regret for not being able to rejoin his three Amhadhri for the afternoon training, he had business to attend, and though he could not change the rules for all of the Marked, he would contest them where he could for Anelta's sake. She had said that her husband was wont to spend a few days in town. Khantara could not be away from his people for more than a day; they depended upon his counsel and leadership, the Mivaari depended upon his lessons and judgment, his Amhadhri depended upon his training and company, but here was now another he could not abandon. He would have brought her with him to the Haanta settlement as his honoured guest if he were sure of her husband's absence for more than a day, but as there was no knowledge of his return, he must make an extended visit for as long as was allowable.

While Anelta was rapt in the novelty of her sandaled feet, tripping over herself and laughing at how absurd she must have looked by gaping at her feet whilst walking, Khantara looked to the wren on her shoulder and summoned him to his outstretched hand. "I have another task for you, Bhontaa," he smiled at the bird. "There is a message you must carry to the Haanta settlement."

The wren lifted his chest and ruffled his feathers proudly.

"You must go to the barracks and tell my Amhadhri that I will not be able to teach them this evening."

The wren nearly flew away, eager to fulfill his master's wishes, when his talons were caught between the giant's thumb and forefinger.

"They cannot understand you as I can, Bhontaa," said Khantara, releasing his friend. "Take this to them. They will know what it means."

He reached around to his back and from beneath his cloak pulled a long striated feather. Its appearance gave some surprise to the small wren, as the feather was much larger than he was, but Khantara quietly assured him that the feather had been a gift from a previous companion and was not taken unjustly. He thanked the wren as he placed the feather in his beak and sent him off, considering if the blue bird would be as generous with his feathers as other companions before him had been.

Anelta, still captivated by her own sense of mystification as to the enthralling visit at the markets, had only enough attention to divide to hear half of what the giant said to the wren. She knew she heard a few words she did not recognize, but rather than endeavour to pronounce them, she asked, "May I ask about that feather you gave to the bird?"

"Haa," the giant's voice rumbled in fond reverie. "It belonged to someone I had as my companion for many years. Among my people, when our companions, or Anonnaa, pass on, they leave us remembrances so that we may look at them and be thankful that we merited their companionship." Khantara's gaze lowered and he managed a small smile. "He left all of his feathers to me. Once we are inside, I will show you where I keep them."

She hoped, and yet did not hope, that what he wished to show her were in a more precarious place, but she realized that in welcoming the giant to her home, she would have to brook watching him remove his cloak. She had a slender idea of what she should discover there; she had felt his form when she fell against him and hardly found what she felt to be disagreeable. He *was* a warrior, unlike the Thellisian guardsmen she had learned to fear and avoid, and with a companion so colossal and foreboding, she could only conjecture as to what her husband might say upon seeing such a creature in his household. She had some apprehensions on the side of inviting him in; though she lived in the home, it did not belong to her, nor was any possession within its walls hers, but he had been so obliging and forthcoming with her, she could not very well allow him to remain outside the boundaries of the small disheveled gate. As they came to the path that led to the house, she regarded the giant's features—his scarred skin, his yellow and black eyes, his broad and rounded shoulders—and confessed that she found everything to admire in his aspect. He may not have been absolutely handsome to some, but to her, he was striking. His manner, too, was handsome, his air so prepossessing and his temper so mindful—she checked herself before she could step closer to him due to some unconscious conjuration, but before she had hindered her deliberation, there was a momentary notion of her being *his* mate. She knew it was little more than a most impossible aspiration, for she was already bound to one, but yet she was beginning to prefer another: one who had openly professed himself her keeper and one who had sworn to remain at her side until the mate more errant should return home. She chided herself for wanting the one she so feared to remain in town for a few days more that she and the giant might spend as much time as was possible under one another's auspices before the dreaded husband should revisit and all her hopes of flight and salvation diminish with his arrival.

He, too, began to have disquieting thoughts on the subject. She, who was so docile and affable, was imprisoned by her own people; she, who was so eager to learn and so pleasantly inquisitive, hidden away and shut up, never permitted to learn or enrich her mind. She was of quick understanding and excellent intelligence—he could see no faults here, and yet Thellis said there were enough to excommunicate her from the world. There must be some mistake was all that he could conceive. She showed no impediments of speech or responsiveness, he saw no fault in her appearance or humour. He felt that her difficulty was in being too attractive for one whom Thellis considered so decidedly low. To see her so exultant over so small a thing as having food to bring to her home and sandals to wear upon her feet discomposed him excessively. He began to think that he *could not* leave her, for if he did, she should surely perish the next time her husband decided to remain in town. She would have something about her feet now to protect her on that account, but her clothing was so thin and frayed, and if what she now held in her hands was the last of her collection, she should be unable to venture outside in the colder months. All these considerations rushed on him as they came to the house, and just as he was about to ask why such wondrous perfection had been so tainted by the brand on her neck, he was interrupted by Anelta saying:

"Please, won't you come inside for a little while?" She smiled momentarily, and then in a voice half-timid and half-demure said, "I know that the house is not so very nice, but it's clean inside. I cleaned everything myself this morning. I hope you will not find it too—" She was silenced by the tip of the giant's finger pressing against her lips. He was touching her again, and this time it was no pressing of the hand but a browsing of her mouth. The sensation of his rough thumb abrading along her full lower lip roused some feelings she was diffident to admit. Her knees weakened, her tall frame tremulous with agitation and senseless joy, and she was moved to close her eyes and succumb to deep inhalations to recollect herself. She failed, however; the instant her eyes closed, her legs gave way, she dropped the items in her hands, and she began plummeting to the ground when a hand, an arm, and then a cloak stopped her. She felt an immense and mighty arm wrap round her to hold her in place, and she felt the cloak against her cheek as her face pressed against him. Before she could regain herself, she was being helped to her feet by a powerful grip seizing her forearm.

"Are you well, Anelta?" came the giant's sonorous voice.

She was against him. Her hands gripped the heavy fabric of his cloak to right herself, and in looking up, she was caught by the look of concern in his distinguishing features: the bending of his brow, the fretfulness of his deep-set eyes, the looks he accorded her that spoke his anxiety. Here was a new worry to tempt her powers of timidity: his assisting her was endearing, and when she removed her hands, stepped away, and watched the giant gather her effects from the ground, she was besieged by feelings her heart was ashamed of suffering. She liked him, and more than a married Marked should like any man other than the one to whom she was bound. He handed her dresses to her, he smiled at her, and she liked him. Acknowledging such sentiments of budding attachment were duly vexatious, but it was an exuberant distress, and she would much rather have felt it than not.

"I am well," she whispered once she could speak. "Thank you, sir, for your kindness."

"Khantara," he slowly repeated. "Do not be afraid to call me by this name."

"Yes—" but the designation of sir that would have followed was replaced with a wistful and inhibited, "Khantara."

The giant made an approving hum and inclined his head to acknowledge his Amghari title being addressed to him. She iterated his actions, he supposed out of gratitude for his saving her from a most mortifying fall, but the imprint left in the folds of his cloak were short remembrances of a pleasing tenor. The more frequent her visits against him, the more he enjoyed her being there, and he surmised that the more time they should spend in one another's company, the more peril there was of his growing partial to her. He decided, therefore, to ask for the use of the well beside the house, and placed everything that was secured within the bend of his arm upon the front step.

"Of course you may," said Anelta. "But there really is no need. I must clean the house every day even if no one has been in it. It's part of my chores."

"Perhaps," said Khantara, walking to the small well and lifting the bucket from the winch. "But my people must wash their feet before entering the home of another." He lifted his feet one by one and began pouring the water over his sole in gentle intervals. "A home shared by mates is a scared temple. To be given permission to enter it is a great honour. Just as we wash our hands and feet before entering the temple, we do the same with the home." He knew that there was little consecration to be found within such a home as the one before him, but he must adhere to all regulations whether in Haanta territory or not to be the example.

Anelta rather enjoyed this notion of enforced purity; she had always been used to clean her residence to erase the tracks left by her husband upon his entering the house, upon his kicking up his feet and resting them on the table, upon his dragging his boots across the floor to take them over to the fire when it rained. This was a welcome custom, and she was about to thank the giant for his courtesy when she looked down to see the bottom of the giant's feet burnt to a black. "Your feet," she exhaled, worrying that something had happened.

Khantara gave her a heartening smile. "Our Amghari, our warriors, must endure many difficult training rituals before being instated in our armed forces. One of them is called Khi-Dhanlaas. The translation in your language would be 'fire-walking'."

Anelta grimaced to think of what so precarious a practice entailed. "Is it painful?"

"It is, but it has its purpose. We walk along beds of searing stone and do this until the soles of our feet are numb. Our healers place a salve onto our feet to help them heal, and then we begin the process again."

"But why would you harm yourselves?"

Khantara regarded the brand on Anelta's neck and said, "To strengthen us. If we are afraid of pain, we will be afraid of battle. The Haanta Amghari are chosen to be warriors because our only fear is of failing to protect our home. We do this to our feet so that we do not have to fear difficult terrain when venturing to the mainland. We abrade our skin to protect us from minor wounds." He held up his arm and peeled back his Dhanna to expose his forearm, the skin thereof resembling the appearance of smooth stone. "Our movements are not hindered by armour this way."

There was gallantry and intrepidness in such practices, and though his body had been shaped and scarred, Anelta observed that he seemed to be little bothered by the severity of the pain he may have suffered. She stared at him, and did so until long after his lesson was over. So much to adulate and esteem, and yet he commanded no respect from her, not in her addresses to him, not in her gesticulations, not even in her upward glances. He spoke and dictated as if she were equal to anything, and her heart fluttered with sanguine delight to open the front door to the house and have him follow her.

A Bird's-Eye View

With great alacrity did the wren fly through the slender lane and over the boundaries of the Haanta settlement, his flight ever hastened by his high spirits and roused desire to obey and fulfill his master's command. He had been a solitary bird, the only fey wren who had been used to frequent the small fountain at the Thellisian marketplace from the multitude of other birds he had been wont to see. His presence had been a novelty when he was arrived to make a nest for himself somewhere less dry than the southern border of Lucentia, but over time, his presence at the fountain had grown irksome to some of the male goshawks. His feathers were far too blue and far too attractive for comfort, and where he had been once met with cordiality by all the birds of the fountain, he was soon been made to suffer the sharp looks of any threatened male in the area. Though he did have interest in discovering a mate, his main object was to make a friend, one with whom he could enjoy common raillery and spring mornings, and one with whom he could be unpretending and guileless with his opinions.

He was at first confused when Khantara had called to him; the voice was resonant and so unlike the nattering, small voices of his kinsmen. He had gone in the direction of the voice merely to determine whose voice it was, and when he realized he was flying toward a dark grey moving tree with grey leaves and black bark, he was instantly intrigued by the prospect. He could use the talking tree as a shelter, ask it to share its grubs, use its grey leaves to make a nest, but the moment he was applied to for assistance, all his notions of making the tree his benefactor ceased. He would have to earn the tree's benediction. It would not be a fellowship easily attained, but to secure such a connection as a reward for his fidelity was all his secret delectation. He would deliver this message to the tree's three Amhadhri, whom he assumed were three lesser trees, and he would succeed if only to quiet the chirping assertions of the passing birds, declaring that he was unworthy to hold such a fine feather in his beak.

The birds within the settlement, chirping at him against the humming din of the Haanta scriptures being sung from the temple and the procession of bards, were even more vehement in their protestations. Who was *he* to be carrying their friend's prized feather, one which they themselves had never been allowed to carry? They, who had been the giant's trusted companions and confidants since his coming to the mainland, superseded and supplanted by one estranged wren. It was not to be borne, his gliding by them and mocking them with such an award to display. They would have him know their displeasure. How offensive to gloat and boast his being considered for the one position for which they had all been trying.

The wren flew through the settlement, remaining well above the trees, his paces never abating as he looked down to view the varying coloured trees, all engaged in their various activities and exertions throughout the assorted nooks of the place. He could not help but observe that only the males below seemed to be trees, and the females seemed to be quite something else. They resembled the something elses that he had seen walking about the marketplace, only these had differing barks, almost no two of them alike, while their leaves were mostly white, grey or black. They decorated themselves with shells and trinkets, lined their leaves with dried flowers, and preened themselves with strange bristly articles passed along their boughs and across their bark. They were an odd race to him: never had he seen trees walk about so freely. He had been used to see their roots planted and their trunks still, but here they moved and walked about as the elves in Lucentia did. Their trills and chirps were unlike those of Khantara: some of the females sang melodious songs, some of the male trees hummed with them, and the rest chirruped to one another with tinkling sounds and made wide smiles with their beaks. He had been used to think trees did not have beaks; he knew that elves in Lucentia had mouths, but as these were trees, they could not have lips as others did. They sang so well and chirped so clearly; they must have beaks to make such tonal sounds. Perhaps they were not trees after all: the females wore silks over their bark and the men wore linens around their trunks. This was all most extraordinary, but it was not unwelcome. A change from Lucentia was what he wanted and a change is what he received.

Even more curious were the hundred or so males bending their trunks and flexing their boughs in the large field he reached at the end of the main avenue of the settlement. There were various implements about the yard, meant to grant them greater strength and durability, but he little understood the purpose of these contrivances though everyone seemed to be engaged with using them. He flew lower to assess this odd procession of movements and garnered some attention as he glided between a line of targets. He heard the whirring buzz of bees about him and suddenly lifted out of the way of an arrow landing in the target below him. He weaved and bobbed, dodging the various arrows seemingly coming to strike him, and to salvage the feather in his beak and save himself, he flew to the large construction at the far end of the yard, outfitted with weapons of gleaming metal and shaped redwood. There were strident sounds emanating from within the building: the grinding of metal against stone, the hammer of wood being borne into wood, but regardless of the unpleasant clatter, he perched atop the entranceway and wondered where he was to find these Amhadhri. *They* ought to find *him*, as Khantara had given him so little in the way of a description to follow, but soon he heard the word *Amhadhri* called out to one of the rather small trees near the targets, fingers were pointed in his direction, and the small tree with sienna bark and white feathers turned to him with a most concerned expression.

He Who is Concerned

Jhiaanta called out for his students to continue their Esbhostaas practice while he inched toward the barracks, remarking the singular blue wren sitting upon the lintel of the garrison entrance. The daring of the bird and how it flew without direction or sense through the targets as he and his students had fired their arrows intrigued him. Perhaps that the bird was injured and could not propel itself from the loss of a wing. He lowered his longbow and commanded his students to do the same until one of them noted the long striped feather in the bird's beak and drew his teacher's attention to it.

In seeing the particular feather, Jhiaanta felt an immediate distress rush on him. His heart became more oppressed as he walked closer to the barracks to where the bird ended its journey. There was only one method by which the wren could have obtained such a rare trinket, and if Khantara had given it to him, the situation could not be favourable. Seeing that feather parted from his Odaibha's axe meant only one thing, and the moment Jhiaanta observed it and the bird's strange composure, he was prepared to go in quest of his master.

"Take me to him," he said to the bird, restringing his bow with haste. "Fly ahead of me and show me where he is."

The wren made a small chirp in reply and flitted away from the garrison, gliding in the direction of the Thellisian settlement.

Jhiaanta raised his hand to his brow and narrowed his gaze to discern the small bird floating under the rays of the early afternoon sun. Once he deciphered in which direction the bird was headed, he reclaimed his quiver from beside the main target, promised his students that he would return in time for their evening meditations, and hastened after the bird until a shout from Bhaaldhena coming from the small clearing set aside for Hophsaas practice hindered him. He turned back and gave a start to see his two brothers engaged with one another in vicious combat, Bhaaldhena grappling and tossing Mhardhosa onto the ground and Mhardhosa kicking his way out of the hold as Bhaaldhena leapt upon him.

Both of the wrestling Amhadhri had noticed the wren flying overhead, and though each understood the message that the sight of such a feather conveyed, each of them treated it with little more than a momentary glance; Mhardhosa was too much in a heightened state of rage to mind at present, and Bhaaldhena was too eager to win this round of Hophsaas and prove his superior might. He had just secured Mhardhosa under his knee when he saw Jhiaanta following the bird. He had an instant to sigh, lament of Jhiaanta's overly concerned nature, make certain his grasp around Mhardhosa's neck was tight enough, and then call out, "There is no need, Jhiaanta," to stop him.

His first consideration was to disregard the call; Jhiaanta believed Bhaaldhena cared too little when such matters arose, and as someone must show his allegiance where it was due, he would go to his Odaibha and do as the situation should warrant. He turned to leave, but was hindered by a fever of momentary agony: should he leave the settlement without his brothers, it might be seen as precipitant judgment, and should he stay his conduct might be viewed as negligent on the side of his master. His leave was further delayed by Bhaaldhena, who released Mhardhosa to allow him a few free breaths and who was now walking toward his smallest brother.

"Leave our Odaibha to finish what he must, Jhiaanta," said Bhaaldhena in a warning accent.

"But he might need our assistance," was Jhiaanta's worried reply.

"If he needed us, he would have summoned us—"

Jhiaanta stood back as Bhaaldhena was suddenly grabbed from behind, lifted over Mhardhosa's head and thrown to the ground. His heavy form slid across the clearing, and the moment he righted himself, he was leapt upon by Mhardhosa, whose seething rage had now reached its peak and would not allow him to yield to his larger brother's prowess. Mhardhosa straddled his brother and raised an arm to him only to have it caught and used as leverage to propel him to the ground again.

Bhaaldhena struggled to gain the advantage of having his immense weight crush his brother beneath him, and when he succeeded, trapping Mhardhosa with his face to the ground, he turned to Jhiaanta and said smilingly, "Our Odaibha is probably assisting the Thellisian slave woman." And then, grinning more astutely with a conscious look, "He has been thinking of her since yesterday. Do not disturb him, brother. He deserves his happiness."

Jhiaanta seemed bemused. He wondered at Bhaaldhena's apparent sagacity until the notion of his master taking a mate forcibly struck him. He watched his brothers tussle and brawl, but their struggle was of no consequence to him. *His Odaibha with a mate*: this was his new anxiety. That his master should have discovered her in such a manner was an endless source of joy and disquiet to him. He worried that his Odaibha should not be permitted to have her as a mate if she were slave to Thellis. How would it all be contrived and how could they remove her from her people without abducting her gave Jhiaanta more anxiety to feel. He and his brothers were young; they might yet find mates enough if they chose, but their Odaibha had lived nearly three times their ages and had never mentioned a desire or expressed a hope of having one with whom he could perform the most sacred of Haanta rituals. Jhiaanta clung to his bow and lowered his gaze, diffident to be the ruin of his master's privacy and hesitant to remain in the training yard when he might offer some help if should be needed.

"We can teach Kaatas today if he does not return for the rest of the afternoon," Bhaaldhena grunted, wrapping his arm round Mhardhosa's neck and pressing his knee down upon Mhardhosa's back. His prey snarled and hissed and endeavored to free himself by grabbing his captor's long braids and pulling them downward, but Bhaaldhena trapped his wrists together and held them down with his forearm. "I will not allow you to win this time," he said with a complacent grin.

Mhardhosa's unbearable and uncontrollable fury had surmounted him during his Odaibha's prolonged absence. He had done his utmost to suppress it through arduous training and extensive rumination, but nothing would do as well for him as the comfort of a full release. He attacked Bhaaldhena on his brother's own provocation, and as a win was owed him for the previous evening's brawl, he would give his opponent the fierce battle he was so desirous of attaining. His rage, however, had blinded his abilities, and once their weapons had been tossed aside, their altercation became a row of violent character. He gripped, he wrenched, he slammed, he kicked; he would be free to expend the remainder of his rage the only manner in which he knew how and he would therefore do everything in his power to overthrow Bhaaldhena and pummel him into the ground. His face being pushed into the floor was the very last move he could endure, and once Bhaaldhena had finished his speech to Jhiaanta, he exchanged a dislocated shoulder for a strike: he jerked his arm to loosen it from its socket, used Bhaaldhena's surprise to conquer him, and while turning onto his back threw his fist forward to connect with Bhaaldhena's face. It was a formidable strike, one that would have won him the match, but Bhaaldhena had been more precipitant by a half a second, had moved aside, and had caught Mhardhosa's fist.

Smiling and rather proud of himself, Bhaaldhena accepted the shock of the blow for the win: Mhardhosa was injured and ensnared and he was the victor. He watched Mhardhosa as his rage began to subside: his body heaved with measured and consoling respirations, his eyes closed, and his ferocious countenance began to fade. Bhaaldhena patted him on the back and said, "Come, brother. I will replace your shoulder for you." He looked up from his brother on the ground to find the one who had been standing before him gone: the bird had flown out of the training ground and Jhiaanta had pursued him. "Jhiaanta," Bhaaldhena said with a disappointed sigh, but his disappointments were soon forgotten when Mhardhosa's became more prevalent.

After a quick replacing of his shoulder, Mhardhosa cradled his arm and stood with a most dejected aspect. He was calm again for present, or as calm as he could be without his usual source of consolation at his side. Bhaaldhena should always be a last recourse, and he was frustrated that he should have needed to use his urgent remedy twice within one day. He was angry with himself, bitter and disgusted. Why was he born with such a crippling affliction was a question which repeated ceaselessly in his mind. He would not call it unjust, for every Haanta male bore his own burden, but to be forced to rely upon others for assuagement when he would otherwise be quiet and civil was an unbearable shame. He lowered his eyes, stood close with Bhaaldhena, and with a grim scowl said, "Khostaas, Anonnaa."

It was said with such indignation and such ignominy that Bhaaldhena could not but be moved by his brother's entreaty. He was pained to see so intelligent and so skilled a creature beaten and distraught, and with a hand on his brother's back and half a smile, he said, "There is no need to ask for Khostaas, brother."

Mhardhosa looked up at Bhaaldhena, but it was a look of wounded pride and quiet agony. He nodded toward the barracks where bandages could be procured for his aching shoulder, and he walked at his brother's side with downcast eyes and a most woeful but tranquilized mind.

THE HOME

So engrossed and delighted was Anelta to be wearing such decorative articles on her feet that she danced about as she entered the front door of her home. She skipped to the side to allow the giant entrance and spent half a minute in debate with herself whether it would not be too imprudent to keep them on though they were within doors. Were her husband home, she should have asked permission, but as he was absent and there were none of the usual signs to mark his return, she could be blithesome for a time and rejoice in her gift. She had been used to think that gifts came in the form of privileges: being permitted to eat outside, being allowed to walk outside of the shelter, being given more than one meal a day, but here was a new form of reward, one to which she commanded herself not to grow too accustomed. She checked her mirthful strides with a clearing of her throat and a sideways glance, and she blushed while endeavoring to suppress her wide smile and holding the door open to welcome the giant inside.

Khantara knew that he must not expect much in the way of beautification for the interior of such a home, but he entered to find it much more dismal than it ought to have been. It was smaller inside than was boasted of from the exterior; the house seemed to be able to govern at least three rooms and a second floor, but he entered the front room to discover there was little more than that to be investigated. There was no den and no hearth; there were only a few cabinets and a basin to one side of the main room and a small table with two chairs to the other. He was meant to understand this as the kitchen, though he knew there was sometimes a scullery and larder to be found, but here there seemed to be a dearth of everything. The ornamentation was also wanting for a regular Thellisian habitation; he was astonished to find that Anelta's home had even less trimmings than his own: there were no furs, no carpets, no trinkets of personalization, no hanging works of art and no carvings in the wooden walls. There was only plainness and simplicity, but it was a simplicity with an air of poverty rather than one of humbleness. Even the measuring of space was lacking in some way: the kitchen was ample enough for sitting and general movement, but the hall leading to the singular room at the back of the house was confined and narrow, the room itself from what he had within his view was scarcely able to contain a tolerable bed. Outfittings and furniture, too, were missing, and upon the whole, the entire house seemed vacant of life. He should have mistaken it for an abandoned dwelling were it not for the miniscule garden visible through the one back window. There were a small set of stairs to mount beyond the hall, but his stature would not allow him to climb them and therefore what was above must be left to his imagination.

In was in his investigative state that Anelta noticed his attention to the garden. "I'm allowed to keep a few flowers," said she. "I would have planted produce, but the Marked are not allowed to do that sort of work. We cannot grow and sell our own fruits and vegetables." She averted her eyes and made a slight sigh. "Thellis is afraid that we might begin to sell what we grow and earn a decent income without their knowing."

The horror of such regulations was lost on Khantara; he had come to expect such abuse now that he was more acquainted with the unjustness under which all Marked were made to live. He instead chose to notice that despite the house's warped walls, uneven floor, lack of cheer and want of everything, it was exceptionally clean. The floor bore a shine and reflected his features as he looked down, the counters and table seemed as though they had been newly varnished, and where there could not be absolute beauty, there was a prettiness in its purity that must be acknowledged. He surmised that when Anelta was not at her slender garden or in her room, if she had one, she must be always cleaning to keep occupied when left alone. He roused from his reverie when Anelta held out her arms and addressed him in a meek voice.

"May I take those from you?" she said.

"You may, but there is something I must give you before anything else is done."

Another gift? she wondered, but it could not be; he had already done so much for her that to take more even if it should be forced upon her would be unacceptable. She took the items from the bend in his arm and placed them upon the table, but when she had turned around with the object of refuting another contribution, she was struck to see the giant kneeling to her and holding out a small parcel of provisions for her to accept.

"When we enter the home of another for the first time," said Khantara gently, taking Anelta's hand and drawing her forward, "we honour the invitation with a gift." He placed the parcel of items from the Haanta settlement in her hand and lifted her arm around it to hinder her from returning it. "My people do not usually bring food to the homes of others, but this is a gift that will not perish. Keep this for when you most need it. It will not stale as long as you have not opened it."

"Oh!" said Anelta, beleaguered by his attention. "Thank—" but she was silenced by his finger pressing against her lips.

Khantara stood and inclined his head. "I am honoured to be invited to your home."

The words repeated over in her mind, and soon she felt that she must turn away to maintain an estimable composure. Her throat felt tight, her stomach began to ache, and though her sensibilities were heightened by her hunger and by his ineffable kindness, she felt certain she should sob if she looked at the giant another moment longer. *Honoured to be in her home*: no one had ever owned themselves gratified by her presence before, nor had she ever been permitted to entertain the notion of this being *her* home. To her, this was merely another shelter and she was only its resident, as she was reminded upon several occasions. Her thankfulness was beyond what she was capable of expressing, and instead of pronouncing more bouts of gratitude, she said a most oppressed, "Would you like to sit down?" and turned to place the parcel in the singular cabinet, screening her beset countenance from her benefactor.

The History of the Haanta

hantara would sit down, but to do so, the great axe on his back, concealed by his shadowcloak, must be removed. He had promised to show her the means of the produced feather, but where he believed a removing of his cloak should be of little consequence to anyone, to Anelta its removal produced very different feelings. A slight flourish removed his Dhanna and exposed his body. He began folding his cloak and was about to ask if there were a place where he may lay it aside when he observed Anelta's gaping features. Her colour was heightened, her eyes wide and unmoving, her hand lifted to her breast, and she seemed to be astonished by him in a way she never was before.

She had just recollected herself when she turned around only to be met with a most unassailable sight: the giant, who was kindly and forthcoming, without the veil of his encompassing cloak seemed a mountainous and foreboding creature: his skin hardened and scarred by its ceremonial abrasion, his long kilt torn and draping over his immense legs, his carriage highly held, the overpowering might of his arms, the gargantuan muscles of his back and chest, his tone and definition exhibiting his unmitigated power; all of this framed by his long and molded locks draping across his broad shoulders and added unto it the head of a great axe hidden behind him had instantly alarmed her. She felt vanquished by a fearful awe and now understood the full prowess the giant commanded. Here was an ominous and glorious creature, one whose form was molded by countless years of training and endurance, whose influence was displayed through his colossal might and overbearing shadow. She said nothing for a time, too subjugated by the abrupt transformation to speak, but perhaps an invitation to take his cloak from him and hang it beside the door would distract her. She went to him, tremulous and with eyes downcast, repeating to herself of his apparent munificence and gentleness. A hand was suddenly upon her shoulder, and she looked up to receive a reassuring smile.

He knew what should happen the moment of her accepting his cloak, but he would allow the incident if only to tranquilize her. He placed the Dhanna into her hands and released it only to see Anelta plummet to the ground. The cloak, now unfolded and strewn over her, pinned her beneath it. He removed it from her, folded it over his arm, and helped her to her feet once more. He saw her smile, saw her eyes brighten with fresh mischief, and his heart warmed to know that they could both be comfortable again.

"I've never seen or touched a fabric as thick or as heavy as this one," said Anelta, grazing her fingertips along the cloak's surface.

"It is a material made from the fibres of a plant that grows on the islands. The fibres are woven into an impenetrable cloth called Bhastaatsa. It is then dyed and used for our kansa, the Amghari garments like the one you see here," he said, motioning toward his kilt. "It is also used to make Dhanna like this one. Water cannot pass through it, and it absorbs no moisture from the air."

"Was this given to you as a sign of your rank?"

"It was given to me as a gift by my brother Tarhontaa, and it was given to him by the Hakriyaa, our leader."

Anelta removed her hand from the cloak. So sacred an article as the one placed before her she had never been allowed to touch. It shimmered with a soft brilliancy, undulating from the giant's hands with each gentle movement. Her attention from it was only drawn by the enormous axe attached to a small leather holder along his back. The blades of the axe's head were large and square, the flats made from a black metal and etched with Haanta characters, the edges silver and sharpened, and the poll of the piece was decorated with an array of feathers of every length and hue. "I have never seen a weapon so beautifully made," she said in a half-whisper, the gleam of her eyes dancing.

Khantara took the axe from his back and laid it against his upturned palms that she might see the entirety of such superior craftsmanship. "This weapon was given to me by the Hakriyaa eighty years ago," he hummed, regarding his fond weapon with joyful reverie. "The handle was made from an imprint of my hands and the blade was made with a metal found in the seas between our two islands. I named her Bhrasthihaa. This means songbird. She has been with me through many battles and I have always done my utmost never to use her blade if possible."

"May I ask, is the inscription sacred?"

"It is for me. The weapons that Amghari receive remain with us always, and when we accept them from the hands of the Hakriyaa, the inscription the weapon bears has personal meaning. The writing here says: *Sonnaa vhon dhosaas, eldhraas et dhinaas*," and his voice purling off the blade when he said it, "'That which is peaceful and honest must be upheld.' It is a passage from our ancient scripture."

"You must have been so young when you received it," Anelta surmised, wondering at the giant's age if a weapon of such consequence was given him nearly eighty years ago. He certainly did not look eighty, or eighty by Thellisian standard, for he should be an old man to boast of such an age. He looked no older than fifty to her discerning eye, but the manner in which he spoke and acted, with such sagaciousness and self-governance, betrayed perhaps a truer age than one her assessment could accord.

"I was twenty when she was first placed into my hand," said Khantara, lying his axe along the ground. "My people were at peace then."

"Were our nations always at war?" said Anelta in a more sorrowful tone.

Khantara was about to regale her with the history between their two peoples when a rumbling of Anelta's stomach made him alter his ideas. He smiled at her abashed looks as she placed her hand over her stomach. "You have not yet eaten today," he thrummed.

"I can make something now," she said, recovering her smiles, "if you will please tell me about your people."

With a nod and a slow nictation the giant agreed, and with a gesture of her hand, he was invited to take a place at the table.

There was some concern as to where the giant would be seated, as he was far too immense to sit in such a small chair, but the chair might be done away and he might sit upon the floor, if that would not be so disagreeable to him. It was rather a preferred state for him to be on the ground with his legs folded neatly over his lap, for he had been always used to sit in the same style for his daily meditations and was pleased to recant the triumphs and trials of his people while sitting in so comfortable a position. It should be a trivial matter to Anelta, how her guest sits or how he does not, but in seeing the giant at a more equal level and sitting so carefully and compactly as he did, gave him an air of sanctity. His form, once foreboding, was now an agreeable sight: watching the slight contractions of his fibrous muscles soon became a mesmeric ritual, and the more she watched over a shoulder as she went to the counter to begin her preparations, the warmer her cheeks felt and the more crimsoned her complexion became. His appearance would be all her private delight while she began working in her quiet way, pretending not to be paying the giant intermittent looks of adoration as he spoke. His pleasant and droning voice and his forthcoming manner were attraction enough, but his form gave her considerations which she enjoyed having but would not admit. The hands that would have otherwise moved quickly in arranging a meal were slow as she endeavored to forget such a fleeting idea while maintaining the pleasing sensations it left behind.

There was a certain enjoyment Khantara took in watching Anelta: enjoyment knowing that she was now well-cared for, that she could now eat and not fear that her supply would soon run out, but the chief of his enjoyment was gleaned in watching her long braid sway back and forth across the backs of her knees, the gentle interchange of movements in the nape of her neck, and the secretive looks of which he could not but be sensible. He did not pause for long, but his momentary reflection was enough for him to judge his own feelings: he admired her exceedingly, for everything she endured and everything she was made to live without. His black and golden eyes began to glow with the warmth of partiality, but these were private sentiments that must not be uttered while she was still attached to another whether that bond had been voluntary or forced. He had stayed for her comfort but he had also stayed to make an assessment of this husband. He had a great curiosity to see him, and not only to force him into prudence with regard to Anelta; he wanted to scrutinize his character, for he had an unpleasant suspicion that the bond between them was not only one of cruelty and neglect but also one of an aggressive and even violent nature. So afraid was she to ask for the things she needed and so apologetic was she when told she was wrong that he suspected some great misconduct, more than what Thellis had impressed upon her. He would see how their relationship progressed when her husband should return, and if all his misgivings should be correct, he would have little difficulty in removing her from such a prison. How he would explain the presence of a Dhargovhari in the Haanta settlement would be his only scruple, as for her to be accepted among his people, she must accept their way of life. He hoped that in illuminating her understanding as to the Haanta history, she might begin to feel intrigued enough to learn more and soon desire to see his people, but a bond must be respected and the line must not be crossed until he had evidence of his suppositions. There were few instances of unpleasantness between Haanta mates in his conversancy and all of those matters had been settled by the Head Priest on Mhavhaledhran. He wondered if the magisters of Thellis, once educated on the state under which the Marked were made to live, would advocate for these unfortunates, but an empire that thrived on the slave trade must be aware, and it only saddened the giant to know that they would do nothing. His only hope of saving Anelta now was for her mate to prove so terrible as to warrant her immediate removal and that the Haanta legendry be so interesting to her as to make her consider leaving Thellis in favour of its inheritance. When he roused from his reverie, Khantara said, "My people were once slaves to false Gods."

Anelta, mechanically washing and chopping the greens in her hands, eyed the giant with an amazed expression.

"On the Eastern Continent, there are few beings who call themselves Gods, but they are not. They are beings who create and destroy as they choose and rule the races of humans on the northern part of the continent. Each claimed one race and demanded tribute, and when they did not receive enough, they began to enforce worship and demand allegiance. They made their nations war with one another to see which of their peoples were the strongest."

"How awful," said Anelta to herself, stopping her knife for a moment to sigh and then taking her work up again.

"Soon, the Gods wished to rival Myrellenos, the Queen of the Fey who governs the elves and all of their kinsmen in the east, but they had exhausted their peoples and could not win against her forces. The Gods convened and made a truce to create a new race of protectors for their mountainous lands. They would teach this race to be obedient and would make them indestructible. They created the one we call Jhiadhi, He Who Came First."

"Was he your ancestor?"

"He is," Khantara softly corrected her. "We believe he is still alive, and we believe the same of all of our eastern brethren. Jhiadhi is thousands of years old, but he was made to be servant forever. He was carved from the stone of mountains and was given life. He was forced to serve these false Gods and was forbidden from leaving the mountains to see the rest of the continent. He obeyed their word for many years but soon discovered that he had great curiosities and great feeling. He felt sadness and loneliness for being the only one of his kind, and he wanted to discover the world and meet the many beings he saw below. He saw the Gods love their nations and did not understand why he did not merit the same attention."

Here Anelta's preparations ceased. She stood with her chest high and tried to listen without giving way to tears.

"He did not understand his place in the world," continued Khantara with a doleful air. "He was not given a name or a purpose other than surveying the lands. When war came to the Eastern Continent again, a Fey named Tepu came to the mountains to hide and befriended Jhiadhi. They spoke of many things: of the war, of the falseness of the Gods, of Jhiadhi's freedom. Tepu realized that Jhiadhi was bound to those causing the war and begged him to appeal to his masters. He did, and instead of ending the war, the Gods created more of my ancestors to defend their regions against subjects they could no longer control. One day, Jhiadhi and Tepu discovered a woman injured at the base of the mountains. She had come to make an appeal to the Gods but was harmed while escaping through the northern woods. Jhiadhi cared for her and called her Traala, which is now our word for woman or mate. In caring for her, he became enlightened to his purpose: to protect her and to free his brothers. He gathered our ancestors and attacked the Gods with the assistance of Myrellenos. The war ended, the mountains were destroyed, and Jhiadhi and all of his brothers were freed but not without a final punishment. The last act of the Eastern Gods was to curse my ancestors: every Haanta male was afflicted with a violent rage that could not be suppressed. This rage was called *ethnaa*, the hunger, and it consumed the minds of Jhiadhi and his brothers for many years. They discovered, however, that taking mates gave them *Dhraaha*, or relief from their affliction. Every male found a mate to assist him in lessening his suffering, and they traveled across the continent together in search of a remedy. They made a settlement in the west and called themselves the Haanta, those who are enlightened, and devoted their lives to finding and creating peace. They began making our way of life, and once they were well established came here to the Western Continent in search of a permanent cure."

"Did they ever find it?" said Anelta in an eager and broken voice.

Khantara shook his head. "Our ethnaa became part of who we are. One of our ancestors, Hebhiitsu, is said to have successfully cured his ethnaa and has gained other abilities in doing so but, no one on the islands has learned his secret. He has written a book whose passages we repeat every day to help us calm our minds, but our rages are only suppressed and never extinguished. I have been fortunate never to have experienced ethnaa."

Anelta turned with the prepared meal in her hands and seemed bemused. "How is it possible that you are the only one born without it?"

"I do not know. It has always been a great mystery even to my Themari and Odaibha when I was young and learning." He paused and felt for those whose rage overpowered their intellects. "My people had never known war again until they came to the islands. We wished to make peace with Thellis and hoped that they could provide a remedy for us, but instead they killed our emissaries and attacked us. We have been at war with Thellis ever since."

Khantara had done, and the bowl in Anelta's hands was certain of falling. "I am so very sorry," she breathed, wishing there were a way to make such a terrible reality untrue. It was like Thellis to assault before understanding, just as it was like Thellis to imprison the Marked without granting clemency or assistance. She sighed that it was so and brought the meal to the table just as there was a small tapping sound at the window to take her from her mournful deliberations.

A Meal Together

he wren, having completed his quest, was eager to return to his master in hopes of showing and telling the giant how well he had done during his mission. Upon coming to the house, pushing aside all of the other sparrows and robins who would peer through the window and beg to be let in for some seeds or small fruits, the wren became even more desirous of his master's company when he saw the meal being placed before him: a large wooden bowl filled with fresh vegetables, doused in honey and light oils, and topped with a sprinkling of toasted seeds. A simple meal to most, but this was ecstasy to the wren, who had been flying this hour and did not know when he should ever rest until coming to the sill only to be screeched at by a flock of envious creatures. He forced them to balk at his ardent remonstrances, pronouncing that he was trusted and chosen for a reason, and though they chirped that they would not believe him, claiming that he must have bribed Khantara with a gleaning of nuts or a fat worm, he would have them understand his position. He flicked his beak at them, puffed his feathers, and with a complacent flap of his wings, rapped against the window.

Presently, Anelta came to the window. The side hinge was undone and the wren burst in with strident tweets, telling of how he delivered his master's message and had brought someone with him.

"Have you?" said Khantara with a furtive smile. He made a quick look outside, and though he saw no Jhiaanta in the copses of trees lining the lane beyond the dismal front yard, he knew he was there hidden amongst the more durable boughs. He made a small sigh, shook his head, and asked that the wren place the feather in his talons back with the others on his axe.

"Is there something the matter?" asked Anelta, catching a fearful tone.

The giant smiled. "One of my students has followed my sentinel here," he explained, welcoming the bird back to the table with an extended finger for him to perch on.

"Would he like to come in? I would gladly make something for him as well."

"You are generous to offer, Anelta," Khantara purred, placing his hand upon hers, "but he would rather remain outside and observe. You need not be concerned. He is only making certain that I am well. He worries for me when I am away for long."

Anelta's complexion flushed with colour and her eyes sparkled, thinking of how nice it was to have someone so anxious for one's own wellbeing. "Well, he is welcome to stay where he is for as long as he likes."

Khantara would have smiled at her invitation, but he was too occupied with smiling at the meal before him; the dulcet scent of the honey mixed with the freshness of the vegetables delighted his senses and compelled him to regard his meal with happy anticipation. He waited for Anelta to bring her bowl to begin, but when she returned with only a few utensils and pleas for him to begin eating, he found such an office difficult to fulfill. He then pushed the bowl toward her, thinking that it must be Thellisian custom to have guests eat first and he would therefore share what he was given, but immediate entreaties for him to please eat followed and Khantara grew chary of such conduct. "My people eat meals together," he said, hoping to impress this tradition upon her. "Do your people eat alone?"

"Most of us eat together for meals, if we can," said she with a hint of reluctance. "The Marked often ate together in the shelter." She watched the wren hop along the edge of the table as Khantara took up his utensils and she was silent, determined to say no more on the subject.

He had hoped there would be more to her explication, but her silence only confirmed his uncertainties. "Are you forbidden from eating at the same table as others?"

She said a quiet, "Yes," and then seeing the giant's disappointed countenance added, "but I usually sit in the garden and eat, which I enjoy much more than sitting at the table most of the time."

Khantara narrowed his gaze. "Does your mate not allow you to eat with him when he is here?"

"No. He doesn't like when I sit at the table. He says that I speak too much and too loudly." She realized what she was saying and remembered to keep her voice at a pitch that would have been acceptable to him were he present. "The way I eat, too, sometimes disturbs him," she murmured, "so when he is here for meals, I wait until he is finished so I can do the washing and then eat quietly in my room."

She had said enough to disconcert the giant; not only must she give up her meal to others but she must also be made to wait on one whom he was certain could not appreciate her abilities. To create something so savoury from items so simple was a gift that only constant privation and an active mind could warrant, and with a taking of her hand, a placing of her fingers around the handle of one of the utensils, he silenced all further considerations on this point with a firm, "We eat together," and made certain that she should have more than he would be allowed to give.

They ate in exulted silence, each glorying in one another's company, Khantara conversing in hums of thankfulness and Anelta smiling with modesty between each bite. The giant devoured his portion with closed eyes and did so at such a measured pace that she had not noticed her eating more than half what she had prepared until there was nothing left to be ate. She had been hungrier than she felt, and in realizing that she had taken more than she wished to give, she leapt up from the table to prepare something more when her hand was suddenly seized and she was led back to her seat.

"There is no need, Anelta," said the giant in a tender accent. "I am well satisfied and I greatly enjoyed what you made." And then, bowing his head, he added, "You have my sincere thanks."

She freed her hand only to cool her warm cheek with her palm. "But you have eaten so little," was her halfhearted plea.

"Amghari are trained to survive by eating much less than you have given me."

She must believe him, though she was disinclined to do so when considering what one of his size ought to eat to maintain his condition, but she would obey him and not contrive to make anything more until the birds sitting on the sill had something to say on the subject. They twittered and trilled and would be heard, and though Anelta could not understand them, she surmised that the remaining seeds in the large wooden bowl were giving them some distress. "May I give some seeds to your friends?" she said, eyeing the birds who had quieted when she pronounced her intended charity. "I think they're waiting here for you. You are so kind to stay here with me. I don't want them to feel neglected."

"You may do as you wish," said Khantara, smiling.

He summoned the birds from the sill into the home and they entered in a whirl of motion, gaining more friends from the nearby lines of trees as they flurried about. Anelta had turned to gather more seeds from the cabinet, but when she had turned back toward the table, she was greeted by the sight of nearly a hundred birds, all of them decorating the sparse outfittings, the chairs, and the giant's hair and shoulders. He had brought a handful of seeds thinking that should be more than enough to sate the little hopping creatures, but now she wondered how she could provide amply for so many. She sprinkled the seeds onto the table and was swallowed in a swarm of talons and feathers before the last seed had even fallen from her hand. She laughed and spread her fingers to catch the sensation of being clouded by so many creatures, her fingertips touching their wings and crests, and though the birds had returned to their places once the seeds were gone, she felt breathless in the receipt of their attention, honoured to be blessed with so many visitors as she had never hitherto known within that house.

A Heart Acknowledging

heir pleasant meal over and the washing done, there was nothing left to do but enjoy the coming evening together. Anelta had little idea of how long the giant wished to stay, but she dared not apply to him for the answer, for to ask why this creature of providence had chosen her as his object was an almost certain manner in which to end their conversancy. She would only be gratified and never look forward to the evening's end. She therefore invited him to the only place about the house that she felt was alluring and asked if he would accompany her to the small garden to admire the few flowers she had been nursing.

He agreed and stood with ready attention, prepared to do anything and go anywhere she should ask, but upon entering the small corridor that led to the back door, he stopped when a drearier prospect than the one the bareness of the house afforded caught his eye. The door to the small room facing the stairway, which Anelta had professed to be the one designated for her use, was open. He had not meant to look inside, but in passing through the hallway and contriving to fit his immense form between the narrow walls descried the contents of such a room with half a glance. He would not have stopped, but the scene he observed within the room had besieged him: there was no window, no light from above or outside admitted in the small chamber through a crack in the wooden walls; there were no outfittings in the room of any sort beyond a small decrepit chair and a worn sheepskin blanket strewn upon the ground; and the only possessions that seemed to be hers beyond the two dresses and sandals they had brought home was a chipped wooden bowl with a small wooden spoon resting on its edge. Here was all her legacy: an image of segregation and exclusion. She had not even a bed to recommend her place as a tenant. An old blanket, one which probably no one wanted any longer, and a bowl was all her reward from such a match. The room seemed more of a prison than a privacy, a place which she were made to sit in penance than to glory in her retreat.

"This is where you sleep?" was Khantara's disheartened inquiry.

"Yes," said Anelta, all sanguine animation. "It's so nice to have my own room. At the shelter, the Marked are made to share beds, but here I can have my own blanket."

Khantara answered with a subdued look. "Your mate does not share his bed with you?"

"Oh, no. His room is upstairs." She pointed up the narrow passageway, and then turning around she murmured, "I once disturbed him while he was—" She checked herself, amended with, "I'm not permitted to go upstairs any longer," and passed through the hallway to the back door before she would be prevailed upon to think of the circumstance that had led to her ban any longer. A hand gripping hers impeded her, and she turned around to see Khantara looking at her with a most considerate countenance.

"He has never honoured you with Khopra?" the giant said, relieved that someone so seemingly cruel had never touched something so delicate.

She looked at the hand he was bringing toward his chest. She was not familiar with the Haanta phrase, but she guessed its meaning from their conversation. "No," she whispered presently. "The Marked are not allowed to have children, so he and I cannot lie together."

"Are you allowed to perform Khopra?"

"Well . . ." and she looked down when she said, "if a Marked man wanted me in that way, then I would be permitted, but I would have to ask my husband first." She had a momentary thought of pleasantness: of being in the loving arms of the one who now held her hand, but she must learn to brook these reflections and cast them aside before she should act on the side of imprudence. "I don't think he would approve," was her timid conclusion on the subject.

"There is no shame in refraining, Anelta," Khantara said kindly, placing a hand on the small of her back to sooth her qualms. "Because of my Mivaala as both Odaibha and Den Amhadhri, I am exempt and therefore have never performed the ritual."

Anelta felt some surprise when the giant mentioned his self-imposed restraint. Long was it to never feel what she had heard deemed as the pleasures of a woman, for if he had received his great axe from his leader at twenty and had been teaching and training for eighty years thence, nearly one hundred years to be without must have caused some anguish for him. "Never?" she breathed, forgetting her own difficulties for the time.

Khantara made a slow shake of his head and smiled. "Come. I will see your garden."

Her humiliation had done with her, and the kindness of the entreaty forced her to smile and lead the giant to the one place where she had always been assured her peace.

He followed her outside as the skies were just beginning to alter in hue. The softened light of gloaming cooled the flush of Anelta's skin, and though she had not mentioned the reason for her being barred from the upstairs, the giant could under no mistake as to what she might have interrupted. He had suspected this elimination, for if she had been made to separate herself on all other accounts, surely she must be excluded from sharing such pleasures. He saw, however, that hers was not so much a physical confinement as it was a mental captivity: the fear he noted in Anelta's eyes when she had spoken of Thellis or of the one she called husband was enough to tell him of her bondage. She feared reprimand and public castigation, being thrown back with the other Marked into a shelter that offered even less freedom and stimulation, and she would obey if only to be given her meager allowances. In walking toward the slender garden, he saw with what happiness she spoke of being allowed to keep a few flowers in a sparse garden. He would not disparage her simple joys, but if she only knew the independence and felicity awaiting her were she to join his people, these paltry gaieties should be long forgotten.

What she called a garden was hardly a garden at all: these were not flowers grown from seeds but blooms trodden under foot that she must have discovered on the side of the road and dug up to restore their health. He saw how pleased she was that they were blooming again, and though he listened to her tell him of how joyous it was to be allowed to keep them, there was a sorrow in her speech that must be acknowledged. She must have wished to keep a hundred more just like those she was now perking, and he suddenly felt the desire to bring her to the temple gardens. He knew she should triumph in seeing them, in enjoying their differing scents and hues, but he must not hope for evil if only to bring about some good. His chief aspiration was that the one who granted her shelter could be reformed in his conduct, but Khantara's heart ached as he watched Anelta turn the soil, and his true hopes lie another way: that this one, upon whom all his desire of absenting Anelta remained, would do the unconscionable while he was watching and therefore give him cause to remove her from him forever. It would be a difficult office to fulfill, the role of observer, when he would otherwise intervene, but he was growing too attached to her to leave her even with one who would treat her with only a moderate kindness. She deserved all the care his affectionate and devoted heart could lavish, and in seeing her raise her smiling eyes, the notion of being without her suddenly felt wrong. Here was a new sensation. He had been used to think that he was too engaged with his day to maintain a mate and give her the due attention she should deserve, but here were very different feelings. In raising his three Amhadhri, he had learned paternal joys of which he had never before then thought capable, and in meeting Anelta and learning of her difficulties, he must confess he had never known attachment to a possible partner. He had never noticed the workings of his heart until given the opportunity to express his affection, and in seeing Anelta tend to her flowers, the only ember of life in so dark a dwelling, he recognized his blossoming sentiments for her and would convey them for as long as he could.

He thus took her by the hand and led her to the front of the house where they might enjoy the remainder of their night, watching the setting sun together. Khantara, mindful of Jhiaanta's presence, walked to the line of trees at the front of the house and sat beneath one of the larger boughs. He heard a rustling above him as he entreated Anelta to sit at his side, and though she had not detected Jhiaanta's presence, Khantara sensed that he had exchanged the bough above them for another less conspicuous, making way for the birds adorning his shoulders to fly up and perch, and giving he and Anelta some semblance of solitude as they spoke.

Together with the fey wren nesting in Khantara's hair for company, they basked in the deepening colours of evening, remarking the subtle violets and ambers of the skies and greys and blues of the scattered clouds, speaking in hushed tones between moments of peaceful and blithesome contemplation. Hands ebbed closer and closer together, glances were stolen from the corners of eyes, lips curled in furtive smiles, knees touched, and before the other could regain any self-command, they were pressed against one another's side and paying one another unreserved attention. There were demure words and shy looks, but these were soon done away and replaced with open spirits and happy ardor. She reveled in her hand being encased by his, and he enjoyed enveloping her sinuous skin; she relished his warmth, he took pleasure in her dulcet character. It was a beginning of something, each of them knew, but what neither one of them would suggest. Such open conduct when Anelta's husband could return any moment recommended their equal acknowledgement of a flourishing acquaintance, and if all this had been gained in a mere two days, what two more might do for their partiality may be conceived.

"It will be warm tomorrow," Khantara purred, remarking the darkened skies and noting the twinkling of budding stars while shifting his arm around Anelta. "We teach our Mivaari how to calculate the climate by the frequency of the cricket's stridulations. The faster they make their sounds, the warmer it is." He looked down for a moment to gauge the interest in Anelta's features to discover that her curiosity could not be truly determined.

In the midst of his regalement, Anelta had fallen asleep. The thrumming resonation of the giant's low voice, the warmth of his touch, the protectiveness of his arm about her had soothed her into a most serene slumber. She had heard the beginning of his teachings and was most intrigued, eager to ask questions and have them answered, but the tranquility she felt under his care was one she had never before known. It therefore carried her away to sleep, but she fought with closing eyes, begging her mind to remain awake, for she did not wish the evening to be over, terrified that when she should awake, the giant would be gone and all her felicity gone with him.

Chosen a Traala

Rhantara smiled at Anelta as she slept against him and contrived to give her a more comfortable position, gently shifting her into his lap, cradling her head and leaning her back upon his forearm. Once she was positioned with her lower back sinking between his folded legs, he spied her placid features with a doting look. She *was* a stunning creature: her slender form draped across him, her braid trailing over his knee, her mouth fixed in a permanent and wistful smile, her eyes closed and unmoving; it was a picture of pure splendor, one that had been hidden beneath gapes of terror and slatternly dress. He raised his hand to trace the outline of her lips and moved to graze her cheek with the back of his hand. He wished to preserve such a moment if he could, for though he was unashamed of his open conduct, would be forced to govern himself accordingly in the presence of an errant husband. There were eyes enough upon him at present, however, and in turning away from his resting object and glaring at one of the trees in the near distance, he summoned Jhiaanta.

A rustling of leaves, the creak of a few nearby branches, and Jhiaanta flipped down from his hiding place with a silent step. He kneeled when he landed to soften his descent and remained in the position as he presented himself to his Odaibha. "Khostaas, Odaibha," was the hushed greeting he granted his master.

"There is no need, Jhiaanta," Khantara said in a soft voice. "I knew you would come." He smiled to show his clemency with regard to his Amhadhri's invasion and beckoned him closer. "I have a message for you to deliver to your brothers."

Jhiaanta stood and lifted his chest with proud conviction. "Tell me, Odaibha, and I will relay it to them."

Khantara nodded toward Anelta and looked down at her as he spoke. "This woman is suffering greatly. She is called Anelta, and she is a prisoner in this home."

"Can we liberate her, Odaibha?" said Jhiaanta, instantly concerned.

"She has a mate. I cannot offer her a place among our people until I see the misconduct for myself. True, there is no Den Themari here to judge whether she may be removed, but I cannot allow her to remain in such a harmful place." And with a quiet accent, he added, "There are many who live as she does. I will not have peace unless I am able to free one of them."

Jhiaanta thought he descried something like a warm glint in his Odaibha's black and golden eyes. He would not say it was a growing affection, but he sincerely hoped it should be a semblance of attachment. His heart leapt in senseless glee, and though he endeavoured to compose his features, he must allow for a small smile to emerge from the corners of his mouth. He recollected himself directly and resumed his stout expression.

"I will remain here with her until her mate returns," said Khantara, observing Jhiaanta's quick changes in appearance and acknowledging his fancies with a sagacious look. "It may be another day that I am with her. Perhaps two." He paused. "Mhardhosa?"

"He is with Bhaaldhena."

Khantara hummed and nodded. "Tell your brothers that the next time I send my sentinel to you, it means that all three of you are to come to me here."

"Haa, Odaibha." Jhiaanta inclined his head and awaited further instruction before hastening back to the settlement.

"Tell the Themari I will not be able to attend the Mivaari in the morning."

"I will, Odaibha. Bhaaldhena has offered to lead Haakhas and teach kaatas while you are away."

"Haa," was what Khantara said, but *They are excellent students* was what he thought. *They are my students no longer and yet they still would learn from me and obey me. I am fortunate to have been given three such Amhadhri.* He was all paternal glory, and with a small gesture, he sent Jhiaanta back to the settlement, leaving him with the consideration of how much he wished for his Amhadhri to formally meet the extraordinary and expectant creature lying within his arms that they might learn from her forbearance, hopefulness, and constancy, and apply these attributes in their own daily practice.

Jhiaanta fled down the lane and toward the settlement in a glow of spirits. *He has chosen a Traala* were the words that iterated in his mind until his sensibilities overpowered him and left him with welling eyes and exuberant agitation inconceivable. *He has chosen a Traala* were words to give flight to his journey, lifting his heels with boundless celerity, inciting laughter of disbelief and elation. *He has chosen a Traala*, Jhiaanta's mind shouted as he leapt past the blacksmiths and leatherworkers all returning to their homes to enjoy their evening meals with one another. He had his mission at the temple, but that would not signify where telling his brothers the news was concerned. His Odaibha had chosen a mate:

Khantara had not said as much, but Jhiaanta well knew that though his master was in possession of the most generous heart, he would not otherwise stay to save her himself when there were others whose duty it was to conquer and liberate the downtrodden of their enemy. He allowed himself to skip all the way to the settlement and toward the training yard on the shadow of an aspiration, for though he had been privy to a slender hint of his master's intentions, it had been an indication where there never was one before. *He has chosen a Traala*, and the notion that he would be spending the night away from his people when he never had done so before was all the verification Jhiaanta required. "He has chosen a Traala!" he panted in excitement, racing past Khantara's home and through the lines of trees toward the barracks. He came to the entrance, saw Bhaaldhena and Mhardhosa standing from having completed their evening meditations, and called out to them: "He has chosen a Traala!"

Although he had not said who had chosen a mate, they could be under no mistake as to whom Jhiaanta meant considering whence their brother came. They knew that Jhiaanta was probably speaking from a sense of exulted embellishment, but they would approach and share in his delight. Mhardhosa responded with little more than a relenting look, but Bhaaldhena's features were instantly alight. His amber eyes beamed with joviality, and he ran to his brother to greet him with the most hearty embrace, tackling him at the waist, rolling forward to his feet, and lifting Jhiaanta into the air, swinging him about as he chose, until he released him to enjoy a more cordial embrace. Once Jhiaanta was given leave to speak, he conveyed the whole of the message, and though Bhaaldhena and Mhardhosa listened with ready attention to every word of the story, Mhardhosa's awareness was divided between hearing Bhaaldhena counter the report by relaying that the temple was nearly finished and being rapt in his own private and internal joy, for though it was difficult for him to smile without, he could do so for infinity within. Their Odaibha had chosen a mate, one to complement him in every respect, and Mhardhosa had never felt happier. It was true that he might lose his early evenings with his master to one who would command his attention in the temple for their ritual each night, but it was a sacrifice he should be overjoyed to make.

They went to the temple on Jhiaanta's command, all three of them with gladness in their hearts, Jhiaanta and Bhaaldhena speaking to one another in high good humour and Mhardhosa remaining silent with almost a smile curling the corner of his mouth.

The Three Amhadhri

hen the three Amhadhri arrived at the archway of the temple entrance, they observed the stonecutter, of whose conduct their master had so readily disapproved, coming toward them from the inner sanctum. They moved aside to give him precedence along the stone path, making him an amiable greeting, but all their affability with regard to what they had been considering on their Odaibha's account was soon to be diminished.

With little idea whither Khantara had gone and only too glad that the supreme commander was not at the temple at present, the stonecutter made a curt bow to the three Amhadhri. He seemed to sneer, and with cold condescension said, "The temple is finished." He paused, faced firmly toward the entrance to the settlement and humphed. "You can tell the Den Amhadhri that he may rest in his home in peace."

It was said with the purpose of causing the three Amhadhri some distress, but as the stonecutter gave further slight by walking away without so much as a nod to furnish his leave, yet more discontent was forced upon them, chiefly on Mhardhosa whose affliction made him ill-disposed to endure disrespect for the one who had assisted and raised him. His red eyes flared, his fists tightened, and his rage billowed out as a terrifying roar. He lunged for the stonecutter only to be hindered by Bhaaldhena's immense arms wrapping around his waist and throat. He attempted to free himself if only to repay the affront which had been so unjustly dealt, but he must learn to brook such insolence and calm his mind while there were children in the temple doorway and watchful Themari in the temple gardens about them.

The stonecutter turned back and jeered at Mhardhosa as he struggled and snarled within his brother's arms. "Were your brothers not here to defend and protect you," he sibilated, "you would have been deemed Tsinonaas for what you were about to do. You should be kept with those who deserve that title. What Amhadhri cannot command himself without two of his brothers and his Odaibha to abate his ethnaa?" Feeling proud of his accusation, the stonecutter was about to leave, certain of his triumph, when Jhiaanta grabbed the sleeve of his linen tunic and held him in place.

"Our brother was chosen for his Mivaala with fairness," asserted Jhiaanta.

The stonecutter shook him off and stabbed a finger at Jhiaanta's small nose. "I question the Themari's judgment," he said in a powerful whisper. "The Den Amhadhri knows how to influence the decisions of others. I have seen it many times, and I assure you that when a new Hakriyaa is named, your Odaibha and his partiality for you will not be allowed to continue."

They would have left the discourse there, but Bhaaldhena was astonished to hear such open slander against one who had done everything to secure the peace of their people and could not allow it to go unpunished. He felt it advisable to revive the stonecutter's recollection on this point and swiftly traded Mhardhosa, who was now subdued, for the stonecutter. He gripped the front of his linen tunic and held him close, lifting him off his feet with a tapered look. "I do not know why you chose to disparage our Odaibha," said Bhaaldhena in a low and menacing voice, "but you should remember who is responsible for our new home on the mainland. You may not agree with his methods, his kindness, or his sympathies, but you must and *will* honour his achievements. You were injured by him, but the injury was one you created. You thought you would receive his praise by giving him a beautiful home, but you chose the wrong one to lavish. He is selfless, and you, by giving him an extravagant home he did not ask for, were not. You accuse him of partiality; we should accuse you of selfishness. You tell me which of the two is the greater fault." Bhaaldhena had done his speech and was unanswered. He placed the stonecutter on his feet and flexed his remarkable shoulders, and implied that the stonecutter should be on his way with a brooding pout.

"I will finish my work at the barracks," was all the stonecutter's reply after adjusting his linens, and without another backward glance, he left the temple grounds to reconsider his mistake and to think twice before diminishing the teacher and paternal figure of three trained Amghari.

A few of the temple assistants, with their pretty features, braided hair, and tall robed forms, had seen the altercation. They had little idea what was said between the two parties, but the vehement reactions of the three Amhadhri were enough to excite their interests. It was a general rule amongst the Haanta women not to offer themselves for Khopra until sufficient reason had been produced: a gesture of interest must be made, abilities and talents must be exhibited, physical prowess must be expressed, and upon the whole, the man of their design must prove himself superior than all of the other warriors of immense distinction. They would take a leatherworker or even a miller boasting excellent qualities, but amongst the Amghari, so many men who were in exquisite form and who fought to be the best even amongst themselves, no quarter could be shown here where making requests for Khopra were concerned. Here before them were three such specimens: one reserved and defensive, one seemingly vicious and precipitant, and one protective and unpretending. They inspected the three Amhadhri from their place near the fountain in the gardens and began to whisper amongst themselves which of them would do for the performance of their most sacred and pleasurable ritual. They looked first at Jhiaanta: his dark brown skin, small features, looped white hair, and light violet eyes were enough to recommend him as a partner, but he was small, too small for what many of the Haanta women were used to enjoy. His sleek body and fibrous muscles might suggest his skillfulness, but his redwood longbow was all their glowing interest. Such a rare weapon might belong to someone equally as unmatched as the weapon itself, and they were therefore disposed to consider him as a more than worthy candidate. They looked next at Bhaaldhena: his ocher skin and amber eyes were nothing to animate where his black braids and immense stature were concerned. His overbearing might was all their delectation: his thick and powerful legs, his wide and chiseled waist, and his gargantuan upper carriage were only a complement to his beaming countenance and amicable smile. The two large and hooked blades hanging from his waist recommended his place as a gifted warrior, and though he seemed approachable and everything they could desire, there was something wanting in his air. He seemed boastful to them, but not boastful from any real complacence. It was a false arrogance that deterred them, one which they had seen him employ at various celebrations to garner a few women to decorate his arms. He might be pleasing to regard, but his feeling the need to use this complacence when there was no occasion to do so gave him the aspect of one wholly unskilled in the area that was most important in this instance. They would accept him if he should ask, but he, even with all his powers of strength and size, was not enough to impress them.

Then, they looked to Mhardhosa, and all their interest soon lay chiefly with such a prospect. He had the manner of a true Haanta Amghari: severe expression, unmistakable strength, taut waist, carved muscles, high cheekbones and wide maw, and while the broken sword at his side gave them some cause for discussion, his rare obsidian skin and extremely handsome attributes were his chief attraction. They would try for him first if they could, for they knew of his affliction though they were not well-acquainted with his character.

They went to speak to them before they could reach the entrance to the temple's outer sanctum. They smiled and blushed and said what was polite, but they were intently observing and judging their manners: Jhiaanta greeted them with a bow and a simple smile, Bhaaldhena assaulted their senses with flexing muscles and prideful winks, and Mhardhosa, who gained all their attention, bowed low and said a gallant "Kodhanaas, sisters," to address them. His voice was profound and pleasing, and their sensibilities were aflutter to hear Mhardhosa speak. They began hovering near him and asking him the general nothings of how his training was and what he planned to do in the later evening hours, but he excused himself and said he was engaged with his meditations for the night. He made his apologies as civilly as he could, and the women noticed that the more they spoke to him, the more agitated he became. They knew that his vexation was not on their account. They forgave his manner and felt for him exceedingly: such a handsome and valiant and remarkable creature, with his long interwoven white braids and pained red eyes, so untouched and thrown away due to an inbred torment. The notion of it excited them as much as it did make them sigh for his cause. They would have to choose one of the other two Amhadhri, and as Jhiaanta was so timid and apprehensive, diffident to seem over-eager and too willing to please without being able to acquit himself his supposed faults, they must speak to Bhaaldhena, who, though with all his ascendancy of height and muscle, could not compare with one of Mhardhosa's superiority in temper and appeal.

Soon, however, all their endeavors to entice and lure were done away when the Themari suddenly emerged from the temple's inner sanctum and greeted them with, "Kodhanaas, Amhadhri. I am surprised to see you here at this time in the evening. Long has it been since the last time you came for Khopra, Jhiaanta and Bhaaldhena." And then, with a raised brow and warning inflection, said, "Are you honouring the assistants this evening?"

The women were instantly repelled to learn of such inattention to duty and pleasance, and while this could be excused on Mhardhosa's side, it could not be the same for Jhiaanta and Bhaaldhena. They wondered why it had been so long since their last visit when most of the Amghari went every evening, began to wonder if they should be worthy partners for such an important ritual, and after a few scrupulous looks and anxious whispers, they shook their heads at the Themari, murmured through their goodevenings and flocked away, giving one another chary glances as they returned to their corners of the garden.

While there were many others in the collective and around the temple who would have readily and happily accepted an offer of Khopra from either Bhaaldhena or Jhiaanta, both were too much disheartened to make their inquiries now. Jhiaanta, ever concerned that his powers of conversation or his accomplishments were not adequate enough, blamed himself for their leaving, and Bhaaldhena, always seemingly chasing after his catch without catching, chided the Themari for his candor with a culpable look. He groaned in disdain, as a chance to harvest at least one of the pleasing and doting women, if not two or three of them, was now lost. He might have managed to ensnare even more than three with a few additional muscular contractions, but he had been rejected for inexperience and now they would know him as having boasted the best of his qualities with having little to commend his gloating. He was much more modest and devoted and blithesome than he would have them believe, but his need to impress overpowered him and it would be his ruin.

When the Themari asked the question again, "Not this evening, Themari," was Bhaaldhena's restrained rejoinder.

Jhiaanta endeavoured to forget his faults for a moment and continued to relay Khantara's apologies of not being able to attend the Mivaari the coming morning while Mhardhosa remained beside his brothers in respectful silence. Though he must be relieved that the teeming women had gone and that his mind could now be tranquil, he could not rejoice at their leave. Amidst his distress and budding fury, he had felt a momentary mirth in gaining the women's interest even despite his known affliction, for it meant to him that though he thought himself an unsalvageable beast, incapable of intimacy due to his ethnaa, their staying was a testament that those whose opinions mattered more than his own on the subject believed otherwise. He smiled within for Bhaaldhena's disgruntled loss, for Jhiaanta's invented faults, and for his own forbearance of the women's company, which made him hope that one day, passed all of his decided and irremovable agonies, he might yet be able to honour a woman who could tolerate his inborn adversity.

Awake

orning soon came to the outpost, bringing with it all the revelrous cantation that the birds nesting in the copses of trees framing the lane leading to Anelta's home could command. The white early morning light had only just begun to peer over the horizon when Anelta was suddenly roused from a most peaceful slumber. Hers was a graceful arousal, made in gradations of yawns, drowsy eyes, fluttering eyelids, and the requisite morning stretches, but when she endeavored to raise her arms over her head, she found her attempts hindered by something resting over her arms. She was further astonished to discover that any movement was rather impossible, as she seemed to be wrapped about the waist by one object and her limbs bound to her frame by another.

Once the first confusion of wakefulness had done with her, Anelta looked up to find the fey wren perching on a low bough above her. She smiled to see him glorying in the morning rays, warbling and flapping his small wings to greet the sun and encourage its impending warmth, but when she realized that she was reclining within the confines of Khantara's lap, all her anxieties of being favoured by the giant renewed. She wondered that she had not noticed their position and proximity before, with his enormous chest and distinct features directly beside her, but she had been so rapt by saying her silent goodmornings to the wren that everything that had taken place the evening previous was an indistinguishable remembrance to her. She could remember the giant's tutelage of clouds and climate, but then there was nothing. She was able to remember sensations, all the feelings of warmth, security, and comfort, but how she had come to be in his lap and how his Dhanna had come to be around her was another anonymity she could not decipher. She was almost certain that he had left his shadowcloak and great axe in the house when they had ventured into the garden. He must have retrieved his cloak some time during the night, but that it should be enveloping her and that she should be sat in his lap were points which solicited feelings of gratitude and pleasance as to make her colour in humiliation. The cool breeze of morning and the temperateness afforded her by the heaviness of his Dhanna soon quieted her apprehensions. Trapped beneath the heavy fabric, she thought to shift away from his notice with the hopes of recomposing herself before her flushing complexion could catch his eye, but in her futile and indiscernible motions, she became conscious of her chief impediment: his hand was cradling her lower back, his palm beneath her upper legs and his fingers curled about her haunches. She thought she was under a mistake at first, but a look confirmed it: she saw his arm reaching under her body. Her heart leapt at the recognition; it was exultation and misery all at once. Never had anyone touched her in such a manner before. That he would embrace and caress that which many considered reproachable and contemptible was all her astonishment, and that he should do so when her husband might soon be home was all her trepidation. He was not home, however. This gave some relief to her, and she had yet more relief to feel in finding that the giant, though holding her, was sleeping. She should now have the privilege of inspecting him without reservation and of expressing her secret delight without the horror of him returning her gapes. She deemed his dormancy before embarking upon her close examination: the measured rise and fall of his chest, his still form, his closed eyes all recommended his dormant state, but how could she be certain when she was unfamiliar with the customs of his people? Perhaps this was meant to deceive her. Perhaps this was a technique of Haanta construction, to pretend to be asleep in hopes of luring a prey close. She shifted slightly to the right and pried her hand from his hold to test him. He did not stir. She waved her hand about in front of his face and there was still nothing to determine his wakefulness. Where she thought there might be the slight flicker of his eyelids or the flinch of sudden unquietness, there was only perfect immobility. He must be asleep, and she therefore commended his abilities of sitting upright and half embracing a woman in his lap while doing so.

She grinned with senseless glee and thus began her inspection: the enormity of his arms, the extent of his chest, the broadness of his gargantuan back brought all its usual delights, but seeing features so close gave her unfathomable joy. She had been used to see him from so lofty a height that though he ever leaned down to listen to and speak with her, she could never gain a full viewing of his aspects. Now, however, every attribute was before her in the purest light: his square chin and wide maw complemented his high cheekbones; his moderate nose, bent and flattened at its bridge, accorded him a something like gallantry; his sparse grey brows and deep-set eyes granted the seriousness of continual deliberation; and all of this framed by a trail of thick and cylindrical locks afforded him a handsomeness merely for his individuality. The one feature of greatest interest to her was the large and gaping scar riving his left cheek. It extended as high as the corner of his eye and was drawn down to the bottom of his chin. She was forcibly struck with it, as there was no creature in her limited understanding that could make such a mark. She wondered that he had lived after sustaining such an injury and that he had not been more marred by whatever had given him such a disfiguration. There were scars enough scattered throughout his body, many along his arms and some upon his chest, but none were so large as the one on his face. She was entranced by it, was narrowing her gaze to better investigate it, and was even putting her hand to it, but the instant her fingertips made the unconscious connection with the giant's skin, his black and golden eyes peered open, his lips curled into a smile and she drew back her hand in sudden horror.

"That was given to me on my first Endaraas," said Khantara with perfect calmness. "Endaraas are the traditional hunts in which all of our men participate. One of the hangaara, the large black cats that live on the islands, attacked me. I did not yet know the jungle had entered her den unintentionally. She thought I had come to hunt her young when in truth I was hunting her mate. She lunged and I attempted to escape, but I soon became trapped and was forced to kill her if I was to survive." He looked down momentarily, and then, with half a sigh and turning back to her, said, "I won the Endaraas, but I did not win unmarked."

He made his explication, but she had not heard him. Still struck by his not being asleep, she wondered at how much of her assessment he had seen through the indiscernible slit of partially-opened eyes. "I..." she stammered, looking away and holding her retracted hand to her breast. "I apologize. You were—that is, I thought you were sleeping." The shame of her forwardness assailed her, and she endeavoured to turn away only to be pulled further toward him by a gentle curling of the hand beneath her. She closed her eyes, inhaled, and dreaded to look back; his smiles were too pleasing, and to see them at such convenience was an added disconcertion. She must look back and address him, however; he seemed to be waiting for her to do so with his silence and his drawing her ever nearer. When she did find the audacity to glance once more, she found his features so very near hers that she could feel the warmth of his exhalations. Her chest surged, her throat tightened, and when the tips of their noses grazed, she felt unequal to speak under such pleasant anguish until his droning words arrived to soothe her.

"Amghari are trained to rest in meditation," the giant thrummed. "We do not sleep." He smiled at her, enjoying their closeness. He could, if he wished, relinquish his principles to imprudence; she was so artless and beguiling, and her ignorance to her excellence made her even more desirable. He leaned forward, his mouth hovering over hers. "Your mate has not returned," he observed, his eyes smiling.

"No," Anelta breathed, "he hasn't."

She was ceaselessly oppressed. Would that he were not so near her, she should not be so desirous of what his pleasing lips could warrant. She silently entreated him to right himself, governing herself not to give way to indiscretion, but he was lifting her back, he was grasping her chin, and before she could make any remonstrations, his mouth was upon hers and her mind was in a silent rapture. Her body stiffened in the terror of what she was doing: *she was kissing someone*, and was even kissing a Haanta supreme commander. Such a notion beleaguered her with feelings of unworthiness, but the tongue parting her lips and invading her mouth was attestation enough to the contrary. He deemed her laudable enough to touch, to hold, to ravish, and this must be all her consolation. She was persuaded by his wandering hands and pleasurable mouth to pull on his locks and arch her back in answer. Affection and predilection with a warming glow she had never hitherto felt resonated within her, and she would not have removed from him for the world.

The fey wren, who was resolute in his lookout for the return of Anelta's husband, forgot his office and looked down to observe them. He had little idea what the object of two mouths and tongues intermingling could be, but he supposed that this was yet another custom in which elves and trees would participate. He made it his duty to silence the other birds who would discuss the event, making their chirruping commentary, and observed the couple's caresses with a canted head. The more the tree's branches and leaves enveloped his object, the more she writhed about within his arms. He could not differentiate between the moans of pain and pleasance, but if the tree was bending toward her and consuming her at such a slow pace, it must be somehow enjoyable to her. A strident call of her name drew his attention, and when seeing who was approaching the house, he trilled in warning, flapped his small wings, and did his utmost to gain the consideration of his master.

Anelta and Khantara had remained in rapturous delectation of one another until the eager chirps of the wren and the familiar sounds of a certain man induced Anelta to pull away.

"He is here," said she in sudden alarm.

Khantara had heard the approach long before the wren had detected it, but his mind and heart were too full of *her* to give their visitor any notice. Her savour lingered on his lips, the sparkle of her brilliant eyes had not yet dampened, his hands were still wrapped about her slender figure, and he was ill-disposed to move in such a pleasurable state. She was in his cloak and in his lap with her hands tugging at his locks. His lips remained parted, his thumb traced the outline of her mouth in the anticipation of another exquisite embrace, but the sound of the husband's voice drawing ever nearer broke the charm for

Anelta. Features that were once struck with elation were now checked by unshakable fear, and even if he should continue to pursue her, all his attempts would go unavailed. The arrival of the one upon whom all of Anelta's deprivations and aggrievements depended was come, and now Khantara must exchange one aspiration for another: to see Anelta liberated was now his chief concern, and if it meant contriving every which way to find fault with her husband to secure her removal, he knew now that he must strive for it. She was his, and their embrace had fixed the notion in his mind; she deserved his protection and his munificence, and in standing from their place beneath the tree and placing Anelta on her feet, Khantara was determined to tell their visitor of his conviction.

The Husband

ith a look and a gesture, Khantara ordered the wren to fly to the Haanta settlement and retrieve his Amhadhri. He had little idea of his needing their assistance with one who must be decidedly smaller than himself, but having them at his side might provide enough intimidation as to have Anelta's removal pass away without aggression. With an assenting nod, the fey wren flittered from his bough and flew toward the barracks, certain to find at least one of the Amhadhri there as he had done the day before, and certain to be an assistant to Anelta's liberation.

In hearing the strident calls of the husband grow ever nearer, Anelta shook with fright and held her hands to the sides of her head to conceive what she had done. "If he discovers how I behaved—and if he sees everything in the kitchen—and if he notices the sandals on my feet-" These were Anelta's interposing terrors, soon calmed by the hand that was drawing her aside into the shade of the tree and taking the heavy cloak from around her shoulders.

"I will be here, Anelta," said Khantara firmly. "I will stand here in the shadows and observe his conduct. If he is cruel to you or mistreats you, I will intervene. I must only see his cruelty to determine the extent of his punishment." Her fears had not subsided; she was drawing close to him, attempting to hide behind his mountainous form, but as he must have evidence of his supposed brutality, he was forced to have Anelta stand alone before the house and receive him. He knelt down to her and placed her hands upon her shoulders. "Hear me, Anelta," his voice rumbled with fond sincerity, "there is no need to fear him. I promised to protect you and I will honour my promise."

"But, if he knows what I have done with you," she said, trembling, "he will report me."

"He will do nothing to harm you. A few minutes of his manner is all that I need to see." The giant passed the back of his hand along her cheek. "He will not touch you," he said in a softer accent. "Only a few minutes, *Iimon Haasta Leraa*, and then my Amhadhri will join us."

The three words the giant used to soothe her sorrows were indecipherable by Anelta's ear, but she understood their sense enough to nod and take her place by the front of the house, awaiting the arrival of one who usually came home in a much less strident humour. She had been used to his coming home at early hours from his merriment and carousing at the tavern the evening pervious, and though his fumbling step and rasping hollers were sounds which regularly signified his return, the din of a woman's cackling laughter to accompany his usual clamour meant that she had more humiliation to suffer. She looked to Khantara's position beside the largest of the trees lining the adjoining lane and stood stoutly as she descried her husband approaching from the road leading toward the markets and town. She dreaded his coming, feeling the oppression of his distant looks, heavy footfalls, and sharp demands upon her. She resumed her office of low stares and hands at her sides, and though her heart beat violently in her chest, a reiteration of *He is there in the shadows* gave her a slight sense of peace.

Mindful of being too close to the husband when he passed, Khantara sunk into the shade on the far side of the tree and tapered his eyes to scrutinize the man who was now before him: tall stature, wide shoulders, large arms, and a thick-set waist were enough to recommend his dominance over Anelta's thin frame and timid looks, but an air of asperity, a wavering gait and slovenly prepossession suggested his inferiority in character. Even more a discredit to him was his slobbering mouth wandering over the flesh of a fulsome woman and his hands assaulting her ripened breasts. To see him with another woman while the one who would be his mate stood at a short distance away was a disgrace Khantara could not forgive. Here was attestation enough of his inattention, for what he could easily have by the one whom he had chosen as mate was attained elsewhere and done so with such rashness has to make no mistake of his neglect toward Anelta. Such transgression the giant could not abide. He would have Anelta removed immediately, but his desire to see the husband's treatment of Anelta overpowered him, and he remained in the shadows.

Anelta could not but be sensible of her husband's behaviour. She watched his hands groping and his mouth traversing the woman's shapely figure and felt only shame for her own appearance. She was so very plain in feature and unremarkable in form that she could not blame him for seeking his delights elsewhere. She knew that she was forbidden from any pleasurable endeavors with him, should she have wanted to undergo any such trials with one of his nature, but there were a few of the Marked who did engage in pleasures of that quarter with those who took them in, and though there had been at one time an inkling of his finding her pleasing enough to enjoy, there was little aspiration of such ideas now. He would show her the sort of woman he found desirable, and he would do so not from any meanness of temper but from a sense of insistent disregard. He would make her understand her place here regardless of the pain it caused her. She should not mind his seeking others; she had no inclination to be noticed by him, but it was a pang to see him so attentive and rapacious to one so wont to please others. She tried to disregard his sweet murmurs and violent love, but when it was so canvassed before her and they were so fast approaching, his preferences were forced upon her notice. The sting of self-deprecation consumed her: would that she were capable of understanding what he liked—she checked herself and recollected, touching her finger to her lips to still them, struck with the sudden remembrance of the lips that had been their occupation moments before. Her husband's shadow soon overtook her and she must now lay aside all the pleasant reverie and resume her duties. She nodded to him to greet him and made a polite bow to the woman. "Good morning, sir," she said with a mechanical propriety. She paused and waited to be noticed or commanded, but there was nothing to remark his attention to her; he was rapt with the regale of a woman at his side and did not even look at Anelta when she opened the door for him to enter. "I'm certain you'll be wanting your breakfast, sir," she said quietly, in a broken voice. "Should I set two places?" She waited, but there was no response; he was too well engrossed with favouring his companion with his tongue to attend. She hesitated and then decided to enter the house and begin preparing his meal to spare herself from any outburst of reproach when upon turning to the house, she was stopped by her husband's sudden demands.

"We'll be having a guest," said he in a brusque tone, giving his companion a hungry look. "While she's here, I don't want to see you. Understand?" He made a quick and sharp glance at Anelta to impress the seriousness of his command and then resumed his perusal of his companion's flesh.

It was as to be expected. Being out of the house while he entertained company would not be so disagreeable. She had little desire to see and even less desire to hear the extent of their pursuits, and she therefore nodded her assent and turned to enter the garden when she was suddenly addressed by her husband's companion.

"I could do with a breakfast, if your maid is offering," said the woman with a placating smile. "Maybe she could join us, if you're interested in seeing how much I'll do for ten pieces of silver."

The husband was about to object when his eye caught upon the sandals adorning Anelta's feet. He raised a heavy brow, and pointing to her shins said, "Where did you get those, Anelta?" in such an accusatory tone as to make Anelta shift in place and look nervously about.

"Never seen sandals like those before," said the companion, favouring them with a thorough interest. "They're so well made, and such a style to suit your legs. Did you buy them from the Haanta traders? I didn't think they would sell to anyone other than the Lucentians."

The comment was kindly meant, but it succeeded in only giving terror to Anelta. She had hoped that her husband should be too captivated by his new object to notice her feet, but the woman's attention to them had secured the looming argument. She looked up momentarily to see her husband's countenance crimsoned with anger. He pushed aside his companion, rolled up his sleeves, and towered over her to impress the punishment that was due to her.

"Where did you get those, Anelta?" he repeated in a heated and mockingly playful tone.

Anelta trembled, horrified at the reply she must give. "They were a gift—"

"No one in Thellis would be foolish enough to give anything to you," he demanded, stabbing a finger at her chest. "I know you would never find those at the Church. Did you steal those from the traders?"

With a fervent shake of the head, Anelta cried, "No, sir. The Haanta traders gave them to me—"

The husband scoffed to silence her. "No one just gives something to someone, especially to a Marked. What lie did you tell to get those?

The barrage of inquiries and assertions, his threatening stance and rancorous breath expatiated her tremors, only making her appear more culpable than she felt. "Please, sir," she pleaded with hands held together and eyes low, "They were given to me by—" but when she was about to give Khantara's name and all his accreditation, she felt a sudden and familiar breadth of shadow pour over her. She looked up to see the giant at her side, his features uncommonly stern and his stature heightened by a raised chest. She stood back from him, prevailed upon by an abrupt sense of dread. She had never considered that one so generous and kindly to her could be so terrifying to others, and then she remembered: he was a supreme commander amongst his people. He must have done something to warrant such rank and position. Standing in the giant's shadow, she began to feel fortunate that he had deemed her worthy of his favour, as from his narrowed glare and clenching maw, she suspected that she was about to witness the extent of his severity.

If the presence of a paid companion had not disturbed Khantara, the degradation enforced upon Anelta, seeing her supplicate herself to a mate and bow to his mistress, had infuriated him. He had waited a sufficient time in the shadows to learn all that propriety with regard to Anelta's honour could allow, and now having received sufficient proof of his abandon and enforced humiliation, he would fulfill his promise to defend the honour of one who had shown herself to be a pure representation of goodness and constancy. He perceived Anelta's apprehension of him when showing his displeasure, but he hoped that she should acquit him the use of his enormity and intensity as much as his proscribed discontentment could merit. He shifted in front of Anelta to screen her from the chief of his vicious looks, flourished his cloak open to give a hint of the might he was hiding behind it, and addressed the husband thus:

"Dhargovhari," said the giant in a bellowing rumble. "I will speak with you."

Though the companion cowered affright and agape under Khantara's immense shadow, the husband showed no signs of terrified animation. He only stuck out his chest, lifted his chin, jeered complacently, and said, "And who are you?"

Khantara made a curt bow. "I am the Den Amhadhri Khantara, supreme commander of the Amghari of Mhavhaledhran."

The husband fleered and folded his arms. "And?" said he, wholly unimpressed with titles and words he would not understand. "All of that doesn't tell me why you're on my property."

"I am here to speak on behalf of one who is forbidden from speaking for herself."

The husband grimaced and looked toward Anelta, who was marking their conversation from behind the giant. "So, *you* brought this Haanta here," he shouted at her, pointing to the ground before him to summon her thither.

She came presently, shrinking into herself and saying nothing.

"Did this Haanta give you those?"

Anelta looked at her feet. "Yes, sir."

"Well, then you can give them back."

She had begun to explain the nature of the gift with a soft, "I cannot . . ." but stopped when she observed the husband's hands begin to coil into fists.

"What did you say?" the husband insisted, raising his voice and speaking to her with condescension.

Forced to explain her circumstance, Anelta trembled and said, "I was going to tell you, sir, that Khantara came with me to explain that I was forced to accept the gift. He had told me that amongst his people to refuse a gift greatly shames the giver."

"And therefore you invite him to *my* home?" The husband's tone climbed an octave as he spoke. "I provide you with shelter and you think you have a right to ask others here without my permission?"

"No, sir."

"You do not own this house. You are a resident here, you understand? I took you in and I provide for you. You should thank me, not invite strangers to a home that does not belong to you."

"Yes, sir. I'm sorry, sir," Anelta whispered, her throat tightening as she began to cry. "Thank you for your kindness, sir. It was good of you to take me from the shelter and provide me with a home."

The husband sneered and humphed at the simmering giant. "Take those off and give them back." He motioned toward the sandals, and when she hesitated to obey him, he added a vicious "Now, Anelta."

"She will *not* return them," Khantara's low voice boomed. "They were given to her with fairness and I will not allow her to bring them back to the traders."

"What *you* would allow her to do and not to do is irrelevant, Haanta. She belongs to *me* and obeys *my* word. That's how business is in this house. She's a Marked and she knows she cannot accept gifts. She disobeyed and now she will be punished for it."

The argument had risen to such a fearsome pitch that the companion was disposed to diffuse her benefactor's fury. Being able to fulfill her office and claiming the silver promised her was her first object, but making certain that the foreboding and gargantuan creature before her did not grow any more enraged than he was soon became just as imperative. She therefore took hold of the husband's hand and stood close with him while eyeing Khantara. "Certainly one pair of sandals wouldn't bring the guards here, would it?" she said with a placating smile.

"If I report her, it will," the husband rejoined coolly. "You don't want me to report you, Anelta, do you?"

"No, please, sir." But Anelta's speech was so restrained by quiet sobs that her answer went unheard. She knelt instantly and began untying the straps from around her shins when a hand gripped her arm and lifted her to her feet.

"Do not remove them," was the giant's gentle entreaty to her, and then turning back toward the husband, he asked, "Is this woman aware of your bond with Anelta?"

The husband seemed bemused. "What bond, Haanta?"

"You mean to share your bed with another woman, yet you have a mate here. There is no need to pay others for Khopra when you have one who would honour you."

"Mate?" repeated the companion in astonishment. She glanced at Anelta and then realized, "This woman is your wife?"

The husband shook the companion off his arm. "She's a Marked," he repeated more impressively. "She's my property, not my wife."

"And yet she is bound to you as a mate would be," the giant persisted.

Frustrated at the giant's obtrusiveness and that his morning of sensual joys was certainly ruined, the husband turned aside and motioned the giant to do the same. He flouted at the giant as he approached. "Leave, Haanta," he sibilated in a hush, "before I call the Imperial Guard."

Knowing that such a threat, though easily fulfilled, was hardly one to vex such a celebrated member of Haanta society,

Khantara saw the need for resolution and decreased the grimness in his countenance in hopes of reasoning peaceably. "I will not leave until you have reneged your bond with Anelta," he said, his voice soft and placid. "I have seen enough of how she is treated and your conduct toward her is unpardonable. You will separate from her until you have redeemed yourself. Until that time, I will be responsible for her care."

"You're not taking her anywhere. I'm not giving up the money I'm being paid to house her."

Khantara seemed confused. "You are given payment for your bond and yet you refuse to share what is yours with her?"

"That money is mine as payment of my service to Thellis. I am ridding them of their burden and they are compensating me accordingly."

"And with it, you would purchase other women when there is one here to care for you?"

"The law says shelter," said the husband, affirming his point by stabbing his forefinger onto his open palm. "The Marked are indebted to us for taking them in and we should be compensated for tolerating their presence in our homes."

There was little arguing with the giant; he would not be dissuaded, and his limited understanding of the rights and wrongs in Thellisian society was only exacerbating matters. Perhaps all this might be done away with an acquiescence of Khantara's demands: he wanted to have charge of Anelta and the husband would be rid of her. He could have the giant return her once a month or so in time for the usual inspection, and then she could be carried off again. He may keep the few silver a month he was being given for Anelta's care, or may even give a silver to the giant to keep him quiet, and have the entire house to himself. There would be, of course, no one to clean and cook and mill about the yard, but all this might be gotten over tolerably soon. Perhaps the giant's suggestion would do very well for him, and he was almost on the point of saying so when he observed his companion walking away from the house and returning to town.

"Where are you going?" he called after the woman.

"Grief from the Haanta isn't worth a few pieces of silver," she returned, making a dismissive gesture as she continued along the path without a backward glance.

All his designs on a day pleasantly spent between the legs of a fulsome woman were now lost, and in watching his luscious creature slip away from him, he was overcome with the need to blame someone for his misfortune. He looked to Anelta, who was standing by, her head low and her expression demure, so innocent as though trying to hide a contravention. "What did you say to her?" he hissed.

She looked up and with a pleading expression said, "Nothing, sir. I was waiting quietly."

The dimmed glow of her eyes conveyed that she had done something to ruin his happiness, and now she must be disciplined for repelling his companion and destroying his peace. He lunged forward, gripped Anelta's arm, and with a swift jolt pulled her to her knees. He towered over her, grinning churlishly at her sorrowful features. She looked up at him as though begging him not to punish her before the giant and then closed her eyes in preparation for the means of his disapprobation. He raised his hand, ready to release it against the side of her face when his arm was suddenly seized. He was being lifted off the ground, he felt himself soaring, and was surprised to discover that he was lobbed into the well beside the house.

Displeased with what he had seen and pleased that he had rectified the situation, Khantara made a curt huff when seeing the legs of the husband dangle out from the well. He had only allowed the discourse to escalate that he might be privy to see the one most reprehensible act committed between mates in

Haanta society. A bout of discordance might be allowable if regulated and watched by the Den Themari, but any physical manifestation of anger meant an uncontrollable ethnaa and warranted an immediate removal. Khantara now had all the verification he required to remove Anelta without needing the civility of permission. Seeing how divergences were solved in such a house, he now had no excuse to return her at all. As Thellis did not hold the custom of recovering those with repulsive tenancies, the husband would not be made to repent and retract his ways. Feeling all the exultation the situation could grant, Khantara knelt to Anelta, brought her to her feet, and claimed her hand.

"You will not be forced to remain here any longer," he calmly assured her, ignoring the sloshing sounds in the background. "Come with me."

He began walking toward the lane leading to the settlement, but Anelta would not follow. Their hands were attached to one another, and though the giant was leading her to a life of comfort and security, her apprehensions hindered her pursuit of such a desirable sufferance.

She looked back to see her husband climbing out of the well. "If I try to leave, he will report me," she muttered in dread.

A familiar chirping suddenly gained their attention: the fey wren flew down from the skies and perched on Khantara's shoulder. He flapped and said his hellos, happy to see his master's object in hand, and relayed that the support the giant had requested was now arrived.

Regardless of the husband's indictments and proclamations to call the Imperial Guard, Khantara was firm in his decision and would accept Anelta as his responsibility. "This mate does not care for you," he said quietly. He paused and raised his fingertips to her cheek. "I will care for you." And then, with a slight tug on her hand, "Come."

The impossibility of Anelta's liberation from her enforced servitude rushed on her. She made a slight gasp, stared at the giant with an air of misgiving, and wondered: *Can this be true?* But before she had a moment to answer her own question, the giant was placing his hand on her back, was encouraging her down the path toward the lane, and was leading her to her freedom.

"You can't just leave with what belongs to me!" was the resounding protestation behind them, but the husband's outcry went unheeded.

Khantara would not look back and entreated Anelta to do the same. He heard the sound of heavy footfalls approaching them from behind, but a wave of his hand secured their safe journey to the settlement. A rustling of the undergrowth lining the lane, a yelp from the husband, and the three Amhadhri appeared to soothe the remainder of Anelta's trepidations in one quarter and give new in another.

"Oh!" she cried, starting at the sight of the three giants, and though one of them was not so very large, the intentness of his features and the immense bow pointed at their aggressor added with the immensity of the other two gave her some terror to feel.

"They are my Amhadhri," Khantara purred, leading her forward. "They are my students and they will be your brothers and protectors. There is no need to fear them." He gave a gentle pull on her arm. "Come, *Iimon Haasta Leraa.* Do not look back."

She had a moment's fear of what might happen if she did venture to glance over her shoulder and she therefore obeyed the word of the giant, resisting the want to see the husband's demise and wanting not to see the brutality that three giants who were meant to be her guardians could inflict. She heard a few worrying sounds behind her, the din of disagreement and the growls of agitated tempers, but she resigned herself to the consolations of permitting herself to smile. She was free from all obligation and all Thellisian cruelty, and though she knew not what to expect from the Haanta people, if their manner was anything resembling Khantara's, she knew she should like it undoubtedly. She considered the three Amhadhri with some astonishment, as when Khantara had talked of students and commanders with such a character of endearment, she had little idea of their being three enormous and alarming warriors. She was struck by their impressive appearances and was even more amazed that Khantara should have the unwavering devotion of those who looked as capable as he did in the ways of command and ordinance. She became so captivated by her own considerations that she did chance to look back, but the image she gleaned was not the fearsome one she had anticipated: the tallest and broadest of the three was looking back at her, was even smiling and winking at her. She turned back to the prospect of the settlement impending and made a wistful grin: the secretive aspiration of her heart was fulfilled, and she had only to bask in the perception and accept her newfound sovereignty.

Bhaaldhena's colossal form was enough to forbid the husband from pursuing his Odaibha, but the added intimidation of his flexing muscles, of Mhardhosa's infuriated features, and the head of Jhiaanta's arrows forced him into silence. The husband stood back from the three giants and realized that no Imperial Guard would dare to oppose them. He had nothing else to do but admit his loss. He may have made an agreement with the giant had he not been too precipitant to punish what he had pronounced to be his property, but all hope of bargain now had done. He stood in his place before the three giants, indignant and defeated, and sighed when they turned away to join their master.

To be overpowered so easily by the enemy and for the husband to be robbed of his three silver a month when he had accepted so burdensome a charge was an unfathomable wrong. Surely if the Imperial Guard should make their inspection and Anelta found missing, they might assume that he had been dishonest in his keeping of a Marked at all. They might be disposed to claim that he had married her and had rid of her months ago, for it was in the nature of the guards to profit wherever they could, and if they could accuse him and claim the three silver for themselves, they might drag him away merely to benefit from his defeat. These conflictions consumed the husband's mind, and the moment the Amhadhri turned their backs, he began his ardent demands to have Anelta returned at once, throwing stones at the giants and hastening after them with all the alacrity his vehemence and hatred could allow.

Bhaaldhena smirked when he felt the stones ricochet from his back. He was about to turn around and launch the husband back to his home with a tightened fist, but when the call of "Mhardhosa" came from his Odaibha, there was an end to his schemes of retaliation. He and Jhiaanta made a conscious look at one another and hurried to screen Anelta's view of the impending incident before she could turn back.

Mhardhosa obeyed his Odaibha's command, and once alone with the husband, he was at liberty to exercise the fullness of his ethnaa. He ignored the stones hitting his chest and shoulders, closed his eyes to focus his release, and in one violent flourish leapt upon the raving man, his eyes ablaze in fury and his hands grasping the husband's throat, silencing the terrified screams. He roared as his rage surmounted his awareness and pounded against the man's face, his conscience refusing to stop him until there was no feature left to be distinguished. His mind simmered, his fists mechanically beat against his prey, the sound of snapping bones and gurgling cries only expatiating his fury. A few minutes of uncontrolled assault spent in the throes of rampant violence closed the business. Mhardhosa's fury calmed, he breathed in relief, and he went to wash his blood-ridden hands in the well beside the house before returning to his Odaibha. He glanced at the broken body on the ground, still trembling with the last twitches of life, and when the convulsing at last ceased, he rejoined the party, pleased with the manner in which he dispatched one so unfeeling, yet feeling some indignity that Anelta's first perception of himself was as a beast whose might was unchecked and whose wrath was untamed.

BROTHERS

She had heard little of the altercation, being otherwise engaged with the giants surrounding her, but now that there was complete silence behind her and Mhardhosa was now returned, Anelta surmised that the outcome could not have been favourable. She had some remorse to feel for the one who had taken her from the throes of the Thellisian shelter, but once these sentiments had done with her, she was at liberty to enjoy all the exuberant reprieve that her new situation warranted. Her bond now broken and her freedom secured, she could speak and do as she liked, but as there were three new Haanta to whom she must present herself, she was so much in the horror of saying something wrong that she found herself unequal to saying anything beyond the general pleasantries. Two of the giants bowed and smiled, one of them inclined his head with a solemn expression, and she greeted them with the same civility, making the small curtsy and nod of the head as decorum required. She looked to Khantara for a means of introduction, but before she could make any inquiries as to how she should address her new companions, the largest of the three Amhadhri spoke.

"May we call her 'sister', Odaibha?" said Bhaaldhena to Khantara, sanguine and eager to welcome the addition to their party.

Khantara observed Anelta's eager looks and smiled. "I have not yet taught her enough for her to decide whether she would like to join our people."

"If she has no intention of being a Ghiosa," said Jhiaanta, "the Themari might not allow her to live in the temple—"

"Oh, the temple is finished, Odaibha," Bhaaldhena interposed.

"The celebration for its completion was just beginning when we left. The barracks will be finished soon as well." He grinned, proud of himself for having conveyed the reports before Jhiaanta could do so for him, but was bemused when upon looking down at his master's companion, she seemed unable to comprehend him. "I apologize, sister," he said, changing his words from Haanta to Thellisian. "I forget that not everyone is able to speak our language."

Anelta's eyes brightened. "Are all your people able to speak Thellisian?"

"All of our Amghari are taught the languages of the mainland," said Jhiaanta. "Our Odaibha taught us Thellisian himself."

"Thellisian was one of the few languages never taught to Amghari until our Odaibha was given the order to conquer Thellis," said Bhaaldhena with a gloating inflection. "We lived and learned in the temple, were named Amhadhri, and trained together until we were attacked. Thellisian was not easy to learn while we were preparing ships to bring our forces to the mainland. Mhardhosa learned it without difficulty."

Mhardhosa inclined his head to introduce himself.

"Jhiaanta, however," Bhaaldhena added, smirking at his brother, "had more difficulty than I did learning a few of the Thellisian phrases."

"That is because you were constantly interrupting my lessons," Jhiaanta said with a begrudging glower. "I was learning while preparing the ships for the journey and you decided to see if the masts of the Thellisian vessels could hold your weight."

Bhaaldhena folded his arms and humphed. "It was a needful assessment."

"There were other ways you could have tested them instead of climbing to their peaks and hanging from the gaffs."

"I had to be certain that I could swing down from them and land on the deck without breaking through to the hold."

"Well," said Jhiaanta stoutly, "your examination failed."

"You mean it succeeded."

"*You* succeeded in breaking the masts of my ships." Jhiaanta tried to recollect himself and sighed. "I only began to learn Thellisian correctly when I spent weeks helping the Vhindari rebuild everything you destroyed."

Anelta must laugh at their argument and hid her blushing smiles with the back of her hand. It was an odd sensation to her: to be surrounded by many formidable men who conducted themselves more as bickering siblings than they did commanders. She could not wonder at their loyalty to one another, as their japes were not spiteful, but she wondered at how close their relation was with regard to blood due to their varying sizes, features, and skin hues. If they had grown and learned together, surely they must be related, but they looked and carried themselves so differently from one another that to decipher any association other than fellowship was unconscionable. "These are your commanders?" she whispered to Khantara.

"They are."

"But they walk by your side and even in front of you."

"We may differ in age and rank, but they are not my subordinates. I may lead and they may follow, but they do not serve me. All Amghari, whether Amhadhri or otherwise, serve and protect our people. Bhaaldhena, Jhiaanta and Mhardhosa are all Amhadhri, but that does not mean that they are the same."

"I am a weaponsmaster," said Bhaaldhena with a prideful grin.

"Of close-ranged weapons," Jhiaanta corrected him.

"And I am undefeated in all of them."

"Most of them. And you also boast more than you should."

"I have a right to do so." Bhaaldhena sidled Anelta and leaned down to say in a perfectly audible whisper, "I am the only one on Mhavhaledhran who was given two weapons at his instatement instead of one." He shifted to the side to display his magnificent hooked blades and made a gleeful smile. "No one has been able to take them from my hands in battle."

"Mhardhosa beat you once," Jhiaanta muttered.

"That was a draw, not a win," Bhaaldhena argued. "He broke our weapons and the battle was done."

"Well, I have defeated you numerous times."

"From afar."

"That still counts as a defeat."

"We were discussing my art, not yours, brother," Bhaaldhena fleered.

Khantara raised his hand and the blithesome argument was silenced. "Jhiaanta is champion and teacher of Es-bhostaas."

"Does that mean archery?" asked Anelta.

"It means arrow-catching," Jhiaanta replied, his lips slowly curling into a smile.

Anelta beamed. "You're able to catch arrows?"

"I am." Jhiaanta paused, straightened with triumph, and then added, "And Bhaaldhena is not."

"I teach kaatas, brother. That is enough," Bhaaldhena demanded.

"Is it."

"Raise your bow to me and we will see who will win."

The bow was raised, the arrow pulled back, and before it was released, Bhaaldhena leapt ahead of the party to position himself for catching. He missed the shaft as the arrow flew by him, and though he had succeeded in catching a feather from the tail, the arrow had eluded his grasp. He tossed the feather aside and commanded another shot be fired at him, claiming that he was not yet in position and therefore the first shot should be discounted. He was readily obliged, but he was too occupied with telling Jhiaanta when to fire and had missed the opportunity to redeem himself. The arrow soared by without his notice, and when a third was ready to launch, he lunged at Jhiaanta to even the ground. He had already suffered the humiliation of his inability twice before their new sister and he would not be subject to the same humiliation again. If he was to lose, he would do so in another quarter, one that would allow him to exhibit his talents before allowing any further degradation of his prowess to be proven. He hurled his immense form at his brother, sailing with arms outstretched, and landed upon him, rolling forward with Jhiaanta trapped in his gargantuan arms. They began wrestling with one another, grappling and tossing each other over, Bhaaldhena laughing at Jhiaanta's inability to lift him and Jhiaanta grunting with every exertion he made to flip his brother onto his back.

Anelta tried not to worry for Jhiaanta, remembering that he was a trained warrior and hoping that his brother would be generous with his defeat. "Do they always fight?" she said in a chary tone.

"It is only a contest of skill," Khantara assured her, rubbing his thumb over the back of her hand, "It is good for them to challenge one another."

Anelta must believe him, though the match was growing more vigorous and heated with every movement. She saw how with little effort Bhaaldhena surmounted his small brother and with what immense endeavor Jhiaanta performed to retaliate accordingly. She was concerned when Jhiaanta's looped braids became trapped beneath Bhaaldhena's knee, but she checked her fears when she observed the growing agitation in Mhardhosa's countenance. He grimaced, raised his hand to his brow, and apologized for his sudden discomposure. Anelta thought little of the momentary vexation until Khantara placed his hand on his student's shoulder and gave him a firm look.

With closed eyes and consoling breath, Mhardhosa said, "I am pleased for your return, Odaibha."

His voice, low and gentle, struck Anelta by its delicacy, quieting her and begging her to listen.

"Were you well in my absence?" asked Khantara as Anelta drew nearer to hear their conversation.

Mhardhosa nodded. "Bhaaldhena was with me. Teaching the Amghari was helpful when I was calm enough to assist my brothers." He almost smiled. "Bhaaldhena took me for a partner in Hophsaas and subdued me during kaatas. I am fortunate he is always willing to defeat me."

Anelta regarded Mhardhosa's pained expression and began to feel as though she had inadvertently taken his master away from him. "I'm sorry," she said, watching the slow interchange of her feet as they walked. "Had I known that you were unwell . . ."

"I am well, sister," Mhardhosa softly insisted, bowing to her. "My illness is not one that can be cured. My Odaibha is kind to stay with me as much as he is able, but my brothers are also a great comfort to me."

Anelta felt she had misconstrued the nature of Mhardhosa's ailment and looked to Khantara for explanation. He would tell her everything she was desirous of understanding, but would not suffer Mhardhosa to hear of his affliction any more than was decent. To give them some seclusion for the little way their road yet lay together, Khantara ordered Mhardhosa to separate Bhaaldhena and Jhiaanta, and once Mhardhosa had moved ahead to obey his master's command, Khantara pressed Anelta to his side, wrapped his arm about her shoulders, and in a quiet voice, said:

"Everyone's ethnaa surfaces at different times. For some, our inbred rages surface when we are young, others surface after we are named and given our Mivaala, but Mhardhosa's surfaced before he was even taken to the temple. Only three seasons after he was born and his ethnaa had already awakened. Our healers did not know what to do. They called for the Themari, our priests, to examine him. They succeeded in calming him by having the Rhubhkina sing to him, but this solution was not permanent. His ethnaa overcame him and he was too young to understand how to suppress it. They called him Vhandouhi, the Mad One, and were going to appeal to the Den Themari to have him placed in a separate sanctuary until I offered to care for him and assist him. I discovered that at such a young age the only manner in which to calm his ethnaa was to have him expel it, and I allowed him to do so on me."

"Were you injured?" said Anelta in a shrinking accent.

"He was very small and I was as you see me now," Khantara smiled. "As he grew older, I taught him our meditations and became his Odaibha. He calmed his mind enough to be named as Amhadhri, but even now, being with the collective is difficult for him. He is not able to withstand the sounds and confusion of celebrations or ceremonies, and he prefers to be alone when his brothers or I am not able to be with him. He does not wish others to see him when he is forced to release."

Anelta murmured to herself of his misfortune but would say no more until she had understood the minutiae of the circumstance.

"Some believe that I convinced the Themari to name him as Amhadhri to keep him with Bhaaldhena and Jhiaanta," said Khantara in a more serious manner. He hummed and narrowed his gaze, looking dotingly at his students ahead of them, "but behind his ethnaa is a worthy intelligence. He is responsible for our success in conquering the outpost. Few know of his brilliance, and I have done all I can to help others see him as I do. He has asked me many times why he has been born with such a hindering condition. I have told him: all challenges are meant to be overcome, and they would not be given to us if we were unable to conquer them. He has done well to conquer his ethnaa, even if he does not believe so himself." With Bhaaldhena and Jhiaanta safely separated, Mhardhosa and his brothers were coming to join them, and with a gentle tug on Anelta's hand, he whispered, "Do not be afraid to address him. Speaking with him will help him overcome his difficulty."

The three Amhadhri took their places in the procession once more, and when Mhardhosa had reclaimed his position close to Khantara's side, Anelta had contrived to say something to him. She thought of what she might say for a few minutes and then settled on, "Are you the eldest, Mhardhosa?"

Mhardhosa, pleased that she would be forward with him, half-smiled and made a slight shake of the head. "Bhaaldhena is the eldest between us."

"Is Jhiaanta the youngest?"

"He is also the smallest," Bhaaldhena proclaimed, rubbing the flats of his knuckles against the top of Jhiaanta's head. "He was carried for two seasons, and when his Ambesari had died birthing him, I promised to protect him and care for him."

Jhiaanta pushed his brother's hand away and grumbled to himself.

"I was called to the temple to separate them from one another," said Khantara. "I found Bhaaldhena carrying Jhiaanta through the garden. He would not leave him alone, even during lessons. I told the Themari they could not be separated and requested to train them together."

Bhaaldhena made an abashed smile.

"Is that why you have the same marks, because you were trained together?" asked Anelta, pointing to the intricate designs inked into their forearms.

"These are the markings given to us when we were instated," said Jhiaanta, holding out his arm for Anelta to assess. "They are the symbol of the Amhadhri and they were carved into our skin with the weapons we were given. Our Odaibha has two marks, one for his rank as Den Amhadhri and one for being named as Odaibha."

Khantara held out both of his arms to show Anelta the differing marks, one similar to those his three students bore with an added triangular design at the bottom of the piece and the other a few simple characters resembling the distinctiveness of those marked on his axe.

Seeing such canvassed signs of their achievements, Anelta began to recoil into herself. "You're all so accomplished . . ." she began, but she checked herself and was reminded to forgive her own ignorance and inability. She could not be the same as they were with such uprightness and nobility, but she would find some manner in which to equal their talents if she were given a tolerable opportunity.

"Of course you will be, sister," was Jhiaanta's avowal. "You will learn a Mivaala just as we have."

"I will be able to learn?" Anelta said with instant animation. The notion of her being permitted to read and write, of going to school and being allowed to listen to teachers and open books and touch writing implements burst on her. Such privileges as she had never been allowed were delights to her, and though she must not be too expectant, even the notion of reading a book or writing her own language furnished her with enough pleasance to dance on her toes. She hopped and skipped in her place, grinning at the giant whose hand she judiciously held and at the fey wren who sat twittering on his shoulder. She entertained herself with notions of what she would learn first, which languages she would be taught, in which traditions and customs she would be permitted to participate, but all these delectations were soon done away when she realized they had come to the end of the lane and were facing the entrance to the Haanta settlement. "Oh," she exclaimed, quieting her mind and standing still at Khantara's side. She listened to the sounds of skin drums and dulcet hymns emanating from the celebration grounds, she observed the immense Haanta guards greeting those Haanta traders who were returning from the markets to participate in the festivities, she noted the fleeting hints of women—the smooth sounds of their voices and their tinkling laughter—and she felt quite unequal to entering the settlement. She, however, observed that she was not the only one intimated by so splendid a scene.

All the sanguine severity in Mhardhosa's countenance had been replaced by grimaces of agitation, and though Bhaaldhena was in raptures over the prospect of dancing women and more Abharaas than his stomach could sustain, his brother could not share his pleasure. He took a step toward the settlement entrance and found it difficult to continue. The closer he came to the two guards denoting the settlement's entrance, the more his mind was plagued with agonizing confusion.

"You do not need to come, Mhardhosa," Khantara said quietly, leaning down to his Amhadhri.

"It will be our sister's first celebration," returned Mhardhosa with a grieving sigh.

"And there will be others that you will be more able to attend." Khantara gave him a sagacious look, and then said in Haanta, "She would never be displeased with you for leaving. You will join us when she will have her Ghiosa Bhidhaas."

Mhardhosa's red and black eyes gleamed when he heard his Odaibha say such pleasant words. To think of such a sister, one who was marked for Khantara by his holding her hand and keeping her near, as joining their people and not merely attending their celebration as a visitor was all his relief. He nodded and bowed his parting, turned to Anelta, and said with glint of shrewdness in his eye, "Enjoy the celebration, sister."

Anelta could be under no mistake that there was meaning in his pointed attention. She had intimations from the looks and smiles and quiet words exchanged between Khantara and his students that by the end of the commemoration she might be prevailed upon to decide how she would like to employ her time amongst the Haanta people: as a partial member of their society or as a glowing component of their collective.

The Collective

Mhardhosa remained behind as the rest of the party continued toward the entrance of the settlement. His staying and their going was a matter of course to Jhiaanta, Mhardhosa and Khantara, but the same could not be felt on Anelta's side. Though there was a sundry of enchantment awaiting her beyond the barrier of the two Haanta guardsmen, she glanced back with every step, looking for signs of Mhardhosa's wellbeing and comfort now that his chief source of tranquility was leaving him.

"Will the celebration be long?" asked Anelta to her companions. "I would feel terrible if he were left by himself because of me."

"Not to worry, sister," said Bhaaldhena with perfect ease. "Our brother enjoys his time alone while we are attending celebrations. He enjoys Khol-Bhisaas and Lausta."

Anelta looked to Khantara for explanation, but Jhiaanta answered first.

"Tree-splitting and spearfishing," he said. He gave Bhaaldhena a sharp look. "Bhaaldhena is only pleased because he receives Mhardhosa's portion of Abharaas."

"The Mhojhudenri works tirelessly to make the meal, brother," Bhaaldhena asserted. Then with a complacent smile, said, "I must eat it to show how much I honour her abilities." He tapered his gaze and peered into the settlement. "The dancing has already begun." He took a few precipitant steps as though to encourage the pace of the party, but when he realized that no one had hastened with him, he turned back and made a most beseeching look.

Khantara simpered and shook his head. "You may go," he hummed, and with a nod persuaded Jhiaanta to accompany Bhaaldhena inside.

Jhiaanta did wish to remain with his Odaibha and his newfound sister a little while longer to aid her with all of his useful translations, as his Thellisian vocabulary was the most extensive of the three, or be of assistance with regard to explaining their customs or recanting the history of how the Haanta arrived on the mainland, but in seeing how desirous Khantara was to be alone with her, Jhiaanta was prepared to assume his usual office of Bhaaldhena's guardian and the requisite apologizer for his eldest brother's behaviour. The gyrating and suggestive movements of the dancing Haanta women were enough to excite Bhaaldhena's interests, and these animations paired with his violent love for Abharaas made for a precarious venture of which Jhiaanta was certain would be warranting an apology to someone by the end. He sighed and gave his brother a threatening glare, and with a bow, the two Amhadhri hurried into the settlement.

When they were out of their master's hearing, Bhaaldhena, while looking toward the celebration grounds, said to Jhiaanta, "I agree with your earlier statement."

Jhiaanta raised a brow.

"Our Odaibha has chosen a Traala."

The two exchanged a significant smile. To see their master so doting and attentive to others was unremarkable, but to see him lavish all of his attention upon one deserving creature while there was a temple's completion to celebrate, children to be visited, people to be counseled and others to be governed, meant far more to them than any outward profession of attachment could do. They raced through the settlement, weaving in and out of the people strolling in their path, and said their secret hopes that Anelta should be a part of their collection by the morrow.

Two guards were all that stood between Anelta and her view of the settlement. So much talked of and so little seen: the glimpses of life Anelta was given when the guards had parted to allow Jhiaanta and Bhaaldhena through kindled Anelta's conception. She observed a few others being permitted to pass, but as she was led toward the two guards with their stern expressions, immense and well-muscled forms, and weapons in their hands, she began to shrink from their sight. They watched her as she melted back behind Khantara, hiding herself within the folds of his cloak, but she was soon brought forward, she was being introduced, they were bowing to her and standing aside, and though she still harboured some apprehensions as to whether she would be allowed admittance being a Marked, none of her reservations seemed to apply.

"You are my guest," said Khantara, leaning down and guiding Anelta across the threshold of the entrance. "They will allow you to enter now that you have been seen with me."

The molded locks, bridge of the nose, and tender remnants of his breath all browsing her nape heightened the colour in her cheeks, but her full astonishment came when she was given full view of the settlement before her: stalls and workplaces filled with leather, furs, silks and materials of every variety lined the main road; men and women talked and walked about reveling in the gaiety of the day, greeting one another in a language she could not yet comprehend, according smiles where called for and bows were necessary; mellifluous song and lively music played in the distance to accompany and increase the revelrous atmosphere; hair braided or bound with rings and several shells and trinkets adorned the heads of every Haanta who passed; long wrapped garments of colourful silks were tied around the forms of the Haanta women while the men were adorned in light linens or short kilts; bracelets and armlets of silver and gold were worn by every woman and a symbol of station was held by every man: a weapon, a chisel, a sander graced the fingers and palms of nearly every hand. The teeming hum of festivity was in every clang from the nearby blacksmith as it was in every beat of the skin drums in the celebration grounds further into the arrangement. Joy, brilliancy, inclusion, and mirthfulness were the sentiments that inundated her and stirred her sensibilities. Tears of sanguine disbelief assailed her, and she held her hand to her breast whilst reiterating the importance of breathing.

"It's beautiful," she presently exhaled.

"What you see is the Mhasdhitsaa," said Khantara, gesturing to the scene before them. "This is the collective. This is where our men and women perform their Mivaala every day and rest in their homes every night. We live together, celebrate together, and share everything we have with one another. We learn and grow at the temple when we are Mivaari, when we are young, and once we are given our Mivaala and named, we join the collective as Ambesari, as adults. Everyone you see here is an Ambesari."

Anelta listened to the giant's speech, but it was some minutes before she had realized that there were no children running about along the main road. Another observation more concerning was that she was just as tall as, if not taller than, most of the Haanta women. She had been used to think that due to the towering statures and colossal forms of the men, the women must be equal to their proportions, but here was a very different picture to shake what she had previously conceived: many were of moderate height, some of slender build, but most of shapely and upright figure, and though their varying skin and eye colours were striking, it was their features that overwhelmed her most. Many faces boasted of delicate brows, sparkling eyes, and modest noses all framed by sleek maws, and upon the whole Anelta had never seen a race of such elegant and striking women in her life. It was true that Thellisian women were taller and handsomer than the men of Thellis, but here were becoming women enough to furnish more than one nation with astounding beauty. Their airs and manner of walking recommended their confidence, and their bejeweled limbs and graceful movements suggested their birthright to the wealth garnishing their neat forms. She admired them excessively, and she stood at Khantara's side for some time awing at the different women who were smiling and saying hello to her, treating their salutations with an astounded appearance. To be standing beside one who had been used to live amongst such splendor yet who chose one so decidedly the inferior of these women was all her happiness. She swallowed hard, clung to Khantara by wrapping her fingers around his thumb, and would follow him wherever he should take her.

She thought she should be disregarded as a stranger here, yet everyone approached and paid their due civilities not only to their supreme commander but also to herself. They spoke to her as though she could understand them and overlooked the brand on her neck entirely. She knew they must see it, and if not, knew they could not but be sensible of her poorness in dress and plain looks. This was a new attention: to be the one first greeted, to be the one after whom others sought was a novel occurrence that she had never aspired to suffer. She would never be required to say her sirs and madams after her phrases, never be induced to sink herself only to aggrandize others, never be seen as a wretched object again. It was a reprieve for which she could have never prepared, and the more the men and women of the collective welcomed and acknowledged her, the more tears she twinkled away with averted eyes.

The consideration and penetrating questions given to Khantara allowed Anelta to shy away from forming new acquaintances. After the initial embarrassment of a soft hello had done with her, she thought it advisable to remain silent, for she had little idea of how her language would be received and even less an idea of whom could understand her. Every warrior might know Thellisian, but to Anelta's eye every Haanta male was so immense and prevailing as to make it difficult to discern the Amghari from those who could be considered yeomanry and craftsmen. She knew the traders by their dress and some of the artisans who approached by the tools of their trade, but everyone else who came for the honour of Khantara's conversancy could have their roles distinguished by inked marks on their arms or the lack of them. They beamed and bustled and came with news of the temple's being finished. Everyone was determined to rejoice with their supreme commander. Khantara might have been desirous of doing the same, but he was more concerned with showing Anelta the remainder of the settlement at present and therefore the celebration must wait. He gave his people due attention, spending a few moments with each through the pleasantries of bows, smiles, and a few quiet words, and though Anelta attempted to hide through his counsel, he kept vigil over her by caressing her hand hidden beneath his cloak and playfully tugging on the end of her long braid. She recoiled and withdrew, but did so with more blithesomeness in her features than she had done hitherto. It was all an abundance of kindness that he knew she must not feel merited, and when he felt that his object had gleaned all the attention that she was able to abide, he said his parting words to the crowds of people about them, promised to join them later, and led Anelta westward toward the temple.

"They are all so obliging," said Anelta, looking back to see a few of the Haanta women assembling behind her and eyeing her with secretive looks.

"They wish to know you, Haasta Leraa," said Khantara with a fulfilled expression. His people approved her. There was no reason as to why they should not have commended his choice, but that they openly liked her and welcomed her was all his satisfaction. He gave a few affectionate tugs on the end of her braid and his heart warmed to see her laugh shyly to herself.

They walked along the main road, passing familiar sights of millers and chandlers, leatherworkers and tanners, and though these professions were not unknown to Anelta, who had been used to see such craftsmen hard at work in the marketplace, to be allowed to approach each workstation and observe what every artisan was making was a pleasant novelty. Those who looked up from their work greeted them with perfect propriety and jovial manner, but Anelta soon realized that her name was being exchanged for the Haanta designation that Khantara would attribute to her.

When they drew close to the lane leading to the temple, Anelta said, "May I ask, those words in Haanta, what do they mean?"

Khantara made a slow nictation. "Leraa means One Who is Gentle. Many of us use this designation when speaking to Mivaari or to our young students. Haasta means small. You are not small when compared to our women." He paused and smiled. "You are small when standing beside me, however."

"It would be difficult for anyone not be small when standing with you." She blushed when she realized his intended familiarity, and her shyness prevented her from saying anything more on the subject. She had only to be silent, hold the giant's hand, and glory in being called such an endearing designation. Would that he might keep her with him was a notion to make her even more speechless. She knew she must not come to expect such exclusive treatment. Surely he meant to protect her for a while and then hand her off to wherever those amidst the collective not considered one of his people must go. If only she could contrive to stay, she should wish to never be divided from him and from a society that made her feel so much its equal. There must be a way to secure her place—or at least she hoped there was—and she resigned herself to her current pleasance, secreting away her wishes in the corner of her mind to be thought of again in a later hour when her raised spirits should fail her.

Presently they came to the temple and stood beneath the archway of the lane leading to the temple doors. The large fountain near the garden entrance, the surrounding verdure and the pond supplied with colourful carps were marvels to anyone who had never before seen their equal, but the immense dome at the top of the temple that canopied the inner sanctum was what first commanded her attention. Its deep hue, transparency, glass-like texture, and gold rims made the structure seem larger and more significant than it already was. Various chambers, vast sanctums and circumference were the wonders within while the intricateness of the carvings along the sandstone walls and the verdancy of the neighboring flora were the wonders without. Anelta had seen the Thellisian Parliament once when she was being removed from the shelter and taken to her then new home, and even though the propitious structure was certainly grand, it could not resemble the style and beauty of the one before her. Just care had been taken in the sanding and the carving of the stone, in the plantations surrounding, and in the vivacious wildlife adorning every corner. Where there might be stateliness in the buildings of the Thellisian capital, it lacked the penetrating sanctity that was prevalent here.

"This is our temple," said Khantara, looking up at the shapes of the outer stones with a dignified aspect. "This is where all of our rituals and sacred rites are performed."

Anelta breathed in wonderment, her eyes passing over the carvings lining the post and lintel of the immense building. The sounds of the trilling hymns echoing within the sanctums, the scent of ground herbs, baked bread, and incense, and the prospect of the extensive grounds captivated her senses.

"I am not permitted to take you inside the temple," said the giant, motioning toward a Haanta symbol carved on the side of the door. "Only our people may enter." He said it and felt the exclusion in his phrase. He did not mean to make her feel the pariah in their society especially when she had just entered it, but there were still some regulations he must follow, and smooth away any feelings of segregation, he took her toward the gardens to deliver the principal meaning in his visit. "These are the gardens in which our Mivaari sit and learn every day."

"They are so beautiful," Anelta murmured in a trance.

"Haa." The giant raised his head and inhaled the teeming fragrance of the various species about him. "This is a small representation of the gardens we have on the islands."

"There are gardens larger than this one?"

"The largest one is on Sanhedhran, our trade island and our capital."

Anelta made a wistful sigh and took a few unconscious steps toward the garden's entrance. Further progress was hindered, however, by Khantara holding to her hand and standing in his place.

"Dhargovhari are not allowed to enter without permission," Khantara purred, drawing her close to him. "I will ask the Themari if I may walk with you through the garden."

"I hope we can," she said in a pleading voice.

"He will not say no, Haasta Leraa, but he is the Themari and this is where he performs his Mivaala. I must ask to bring you here as he would need to ask me to bring you to the training grounds." He touched the outline of her face and motioned her toward the end of the lane. "We will visit again soon, but first we have a ceremony to attend."

He pressed her hand to lead her away, but her mind was too rapt in the hanging vines, tall palms and blooming flowers to follow. She was gazing back at the rich vegetation with a pining expression. Even the sound of the music in the distance was diminished by the calls of the rare birds hopping along the low boughs. They tweeted and trilled, entreating her to enter.

"Come, Iimon Haasta Leraa," Khantara's voice rumbled, supplanting the chirrups from his friends.

Her feet would answer, but her attention was still governed by the extensive grounds and few elegantly dressed temple assistants watering the soil around the large blooms.

Their parting was meant to be swift, but a flurry of exulted children shouting in high revel suddenly sprang from their places deep within the garden. "Odaibha," they chimed, leaping up and down, attacking him with embraces about his chins, leaping upon him, grabbing the ends of his long locks and swinging back and forth from them. Some stared at Anelta with expectant looks, as though waiting for some explanation to her appearance when their teacher had been so used to come alone. They fumbled over his large feet, played with the end of Anelta's braid, and when they heard their Themari calling them back to their lesson, many of them hid beneath the folds of their Odaibha's shadowcloak. Khantara stepped back to remove their screen and kindly requested that they return to their lesson, but "Will you come tomorrow?" was the question that kept them at his feet and they would only leave once he had promised to resume his usual character of visitation. They cheered and leapt in the air with hands raised, all delight to think of what they could be learning tomorrow from their favourite master, and when the call for them came again, they scampered away with a "Tagmhaanas, Odaibha," leaving Khantara with doting feelings and Anelta in breathless reflection.

There was something to seeing the giant react so well with those whom others might have found troublesome and insistent. He was easy and forbearing of their entreaties, had taken their tuggings and pullings for their want of his attention, had smiled at their glittering eyes and faces in a glow of heat from having run to greet him. She recollected the faint remembrances of her parents, and though most of the summoned sentiments were loving, she had never been permitted to act with such openness when presenting herself to others. She was shaken from her reverie when a warrior, who was walking up the lane, came to address them. She bowed and smiled and said something about how happy she was to meet him, but she was struck by his difference in appearance: he was not as large or as foreboding as the rest, his skin was tanned but more to the style of a Lucentian's and not a Haanta's hue, his hair was black and braided, his eyes dark and sharp, and when he inclined his head with respect, she saw a set of long, pointed ears. He *was* Lucentian, and Anelta must confess herself pleasantly surprised to see that there were at least a few amongst the Haanta who were not born of their race. It gave her hope and comfort in a quarter where she had been anxious hitherto. The different markings on his arm suggested his not being an Amhadhri, but the inked characters under his eyes gave him an air of higher importance.

"Kodhanaas, sister," said the warrior. "Are you here to celebrate the completion of the temple with us?"

"I am, sir," she replied, fearful of using the same address in return to one who boasted such consequence.

"I am the Den Anatari, chief guardsman of Mhavhaledhran."

She knew the rank of Den to be one of high esteem and was therefore glad to have not addressed him with more familiarity than was dissevered.

"I don't mean to leave you so soon, but I must see the Themari."

"Will we see you at the celebration, Den Anatari?" Anelta felt an affectionate press of the hand when she fumbled through the Haanta title.

"You won't, unfortunately," said the Lucentian with a smile. "I came to observe the Amghari this morning. Now that the outpost is settled, it needs Anatari to protect it, and while we have many of my men from the islands here to do so, someone must command them in my absence. Another Den Anatari must be chosen for Khantara Ghaasta."

Anelta heard the familiar name and repeated the unknown phrase in bemusement.

"Did the Den Amhadhri not tell you, sister?" said the Lucentian, looking at Khantara with astonishment. "The outpost was named after its conqueror."

Khantara looked ashamed to have his little vanity flattered. He made a small sigh and sideways glance.

"He is too modest, sister, to tell you half of his accomplishments. The Den Amhadhri Vhessel Dhoss-hi Khantara has beaten me in every hunt and every match we have shared together. He has the perseverance and endurance of a mountain. Anything you may ask him, he will answer and if he does not know, he will find your answer. This is what makes him out greatest Odaibha."

"Phandhanta," Khantara interposed, hoping to silence the Lucentian's incessant approbation.

A subduing glare was enough for the Den Anatari to understand him, and though it was meant to mute his accolades, it could not suppress his smiles. The giant was too humble and too unpretending for one who had trounced himself countless times during their training, but where Khantara would be silent on the subject, the Lucentian could only share a momentary pause. "You will never let anyone know of your greatness," he returned, speaking in Haanta.

Khantara made an almost imperceptible look to Anelta and gave the Den Anatari a conscious glare.

A misapprehension occurred that resulted in a most desirable outcome: the Lucentian had mistaken the giant's humility as a means of catching the woman at his side. Many had sought Khantara for Khopra but none had been honoured. It should be an effortless venture for one of Khantara's situation to find a woman who would willingly accept his request, but here, the Den Anatari suspected, the giant had wanted one whose good opinion was not so easily attained, one who would judge him independently of his previous merits, and he therefore understood the need for anonymity. "Well," said he, smiling significantly to Khantara, "enjoy the celebration." And then, turning to Anelta, "Tagmhaanas, sister, and I hope to see you again soon, perhaps on Mhavhaledhran once everything on the mainland is settled." He was gone to the temple directly, and Anelta was led to the main road in his wake.

If even those who shared in Khantara's rank of Den were according him such praise, he must be seen as a god to those in ranks below him. Anelta trembled with renewed trepidation and wondered at how many other accomplishments were in the giant's history and how many more of which were being kept from her to secure her comfort.

About the Author

Michelle Franklin is a small woman of moderate consequence who writes many, many books about giants, romance, and chocolate. You can find more about her and the Haanta series at her website: http://thehaanta.blogspot.ca/